PROJECT GHOST

By:
Bennard Terrell

Table Of Contents

Chapter 1: Unearthing

Like a fine blanket that eluded the touch of human hands, a layer of dust had settled over everything in MIT's oldest science building. This part of the campus was supposed to be renovated, but it had been forgotten temporarily — a fact that made it irresistible to those with curiosity and bravery.

Josh, Melinda and Timmy were three sophomore programmers who were not afraid to take risks. They had heard stories about the equipment left behind from years of research. Using only their smartphones' blue light for visibility, they moved through the maze of hallways cluttered with remnants from the past.

When they arrived at the lab, the door made an ominous creaking sound as it swung open. The room seemed like it hadn't aged a day since it was last used. In dim light, large machines wrapped in sheets of plastic looked like ghosts. Tables were littered with glassware and old notebooks covered in thick layers of dust.

"Whoa! Look at this!" Josh shouted as he yanked a tarp off a machine that resembled a large box. Underneath it was a nest of tubes and wires so complex it could have been mistaken for something out of a sci-fi movie set instead of an MIT lab.

Ever skeptical and always the smartest person in any room, Melinda approached cautiously. “Be careful with that thing,” she warned Josh in her usual firm voice that could command anything within earshot — except now there was excitement underneath her words.

Timmy had been quiet up until now; he had wandered over to a workbench where he found several leather-bound journals stacked on top of one another. He wiped away enough dirt to read the title on top: “Project Spectra – Experiments and Observations.” His eyes widened as he flipped through pages filled with technical drawings and handwritten notes.

“You guys need to see this,” Timmy called over his shoulder without looking up from the journal, still turning pages.

Josh and Melinda moved to his side and leaned over him so they could get a better look at what was open in front of them. It was an entry dated back to 1974, outlining an experiment designed to use electromagnetic sensors and early computer modeling to detect the presence of supernatural entities.

“What were they trying to do here? Catch ghosts?” Josh laughed — but his laugh died down when he saw the looks on Melinda’s and Timmy’s faces. They took it seriously.

“Maybe,” said Melinda, whose brain started going a million miles an hour with technological possibilities. “What if we actually could see if there’s something… out there?”

With that shared look of excitement reserved for mischief-makers about to break into uncharted territory, they began searching the room more deliberately, gathering up scattered pieces of equipment. Every component seemed to find its match with an almost eerie precision — as if their hands were being guided.

The lab became their world as the night deepened outside. They connected cables, adjusted settings and powered on old computers. The machines hummed with life; screens flashed lines of code that hadn't run in years.

Unaware of the passing hours and the figure lurking just outside of their torchlight, they were intoxicated by the excitement of discovery and the possibilities of revival. For a second time, the lab was alive with electrical currents and voices long hushed by time as Josh, Melinda, and Timmy teetered on a precipice whose endpoint could not be foreseen. The line between scientific and supernatural began to blur as they probed deeper into the secrets of the abandoned project.

Each part they reactivated made it seem less like a forgotten place and more like an unimaginable somewhere else. What had started as mirth for the trio became an irresistible attraction toward what was unknowable when lights on their equipment's screens gave off a dim periodic light. As if it had been in a coma for years but now was stretching its limbs and unable to keep hidden any longer, this very laboratory seemed awake.

Being that she always thought up scenarios and ran calculations in her head, Melinda connected their phones to the apparatus first; from old circuit boards she'd fashioned a makeshift interface which she rapidly deployed with new lines of code. "If we can detect these… whatever-they-are," she said skeptically yet hopefully, "we might also be able to see them."

Josh stood behind her with his usual enthusiasm—mostly fetching tools or holding flashlights steady over her workspace—and watched curiously; but his jokes subsided when he realized how serious their experiment had become.

Timmy continued flipping through journals which revealed more about what this project originally wanted to achieve before being abandoned: "Here it says everything stopped because of an 'incident.' There aren't any details on what exactly went down, but something happened that made them shut everything down." He sounded nervous.

They sat in silence for some time after Timmy spoke those words. Then Josh asked softly—almost too softly—"What kind of incident?"

"I don't know," Timmy said. "But whatever it was, they freaked out and stopped. And these were scientists."

Their smartphones connected to the screens flickered; Melinda's interface began to stabilize, and a rough graphical representation came into view. It was basic but legible—a digital map of a room, with three small dots showing where they were.

"Wait, is it supposed to do that?" Josh pointed at another dot on the edge of the screen; unlike their moving icons, this one did not budge.

"No clue," Melinda answered, leaning in closer. "It shouldn't be tracking us… It's picking up something else."

A shiver passed through the room, and for the first time since arriving that night they felt a coldness settle over them. They looked around at each other with wide eyes; suddenly aware of what they had done.

They watched the blip move with fear and curiosity. The things around them felt electric, as if they were brimming with invisible energy — a charge audible through static buzzing in their ears.

"Should we turn it off?" asked Timmy, his voice shaking ever so slightly.

"No, let's see what it is," said Melinda, her voice steady though cautious. She poised her fingers above the keyboard ready to shut everything down at a moment's notice.

Josh nodded and grabbed onto a nearby table for support. His eyes never strayed from the screen. It had almost reached them — almost reached their icons. Their world and whatever was beyond it blurred in that stage of technological development where the physical gives way to something else entirely: a shadow at the edge of one's vision growing denser, more substantial — darkness at the periphery of light born by man.

And as this chapter closes tension peaks leaving everything hanging between science and specters; their experiment results could be anything, may cost life or limb. There was so much tension in here! What could this mysterious blip mean? And why was it moving closer to their icons on display? That silent hum morphed into something like rhythm which made me feel eerie while reading through my nerves prickled so hard that I couldn't help but shiver imagining worst case scenarios playing out before them all just then when those words rang out from behind me – "Maybe it's nothing but electrical interference?"

But no matter how casually Josh tried to say those words there still remained tightness his shoulders reflected by slight trembling within fingers held across chest out towards right shoulder blade where stress can settle into muscle knots if allowed enough time pass unchecked until pain begins course its own path down arm along outside edge until eventually radiating throughout entire backside making itself known even further up neck where tendons attach base skull causing shooting pains upwards towards temples until finally subsiding somewhere deep inside brain where nothing could reach except for dull thumping against inner walls only audible during moments absolute silence.

Exactly at that moment a shadow slid away from the corner of the room. It was slight, one could almost miss it if they weren't looking right at it. But when seen, it was unmistakable — a blacker patch of dark that moved, separate and aware.

Timmy gasped and took instinctive step toward the door but Josh grabbed his arm. "No, we have to stay together. Remember, it might be dangerous."

"Or it could be the single most important discovery in all of paranormal research," Melinda added, her scientist brain lighting up with all the implications.

The shadow stopped as if thinking about them and then began moving towards them slowly. Each step was exact, purposeful and unquestionably aimed at them.

Melinda reached out and hit 'enter' for shutdown sequence. The screens went black, the humming stopped; for an instant there was nothing but silence. Then the shadow did not go away or vanish as shadows are supposed to do when you take away their electronic light; instead it came on undeterred continuing to advance now only lit by faint glow of their cellphones.

“We need to get out of here,” said Josh without his usual bravado even though he looked just as scared as Timmy who he had tried so hard not show fear in front of before this happened because both boys always acted tough around each other especially since everybody knew how much girls loved brave guys like themselves – according Melinda’s hypothesis anyway (she had heard this somewhere once during another study). “This was a mistake.”

“No—” started Melinda but shadow engulfed them before she could finish speaking. Cold turned into freezing bit into flesh seeped through bones; breaths came out white puff’s teeth chattered uncontrollably — then just as quickly left leaving behind shivering stunned bodies.

“What was that?” managed Timmy still stuttering with fear scanning around room where shadow should have been but was no longer. He felt cold even though it was warm in here now and he kept shivering like before only worse.

“I don’t know,” said Melinda her voice steady despite her trembling body. “But I think we just made first contact with something… not from this world.”

The room looked normal again after having that weird look about it earlier as if nothing had ever happened at all–except for what they had just been through couldn't forget even if tried because their reality had been tested and even though screens were dark now there was no way to tell how deep this discovery went until later; so chapter ends with them sitting quietly lost in thoughts about what should have done differently, risks taken and uncharted territory entered into.

Chapter 2:
The Discovery

The MIT campus is calm during the late hours; the typical hustle and bustle of student life replaced by cricket song and distant traffic hum. But beneath the quiet, in their small cluttered dorm room, Josh, Melinda, and Timmy are wide awake. Wires, laptops, old borrowed equipment from the lab surround them in chaotic harmony. It had only made them more determined. They had plunged themselves into uncovering the secrets of this mysterious technology.

For nights on end they worked – tirelessly – though it seemed less like work with every passing moment. Melinda took to coding first; her fingers dancing across the keys with such grace that she made even outdated programming languages look easy. She had melded together ancient code found in those same journals with modern programming, creating a functional user interface for their spectral detection app.

Josh salvaged and repurposed some old sensors from the lab — his hardware skills coming in handy once again – rigging them into a more portable setup which could interface directly with their smartphones via Bluetooth. "This way we can take it anywhere," he said as he connected the last wire — a glimmer of pride lighting up his eyes.

Meanwhile Timmy pored over those same journals; finding notes and theories that gave insight into how it all worked. He was particularly interested in spectral frequencies and electromagnetic disruptions as means of detecting ghosts. “It’s like tuning a radio but instead of music we’re looking for ghost signals,” he joked — his laughter nervous at best.

As they finished up their prototype app, they contemplated how to test it; returning to the lab was not an option after that shadow…incident. Too fresh. So instead, they chose the library; haunted yes but not AS haunted as say…the abandoned lab.

The library at night is another world entirely…silent…still…long shadows cast by moonlight streaming through tall windows. They enter quietly…not wanting to be caught…app ready on Josh’s phone. It is a radar-like screen that will pulse gently when it detects a spectral anomaly.

They walk between rows of darkened books, the only sounds being soft pads of footsteps and the low distant whir of the ventilation system. Melinda holds the phone, watching closely as they move. The app stays quiet. The screen stays still.

Turning a corner they approach the back section of the library; where all the oldest books are kept. The air feels cooler here…shadows deeper. Melinda’s phone vibrates in her hand — she jumps so hard she nearly drops it. Josh steadies her grip. The screen lights up. A soft blue pulse emanates from its center.

“There! There it is!” Melinda whispers with a mixture of excitement and fear. They watch in amazement as the pulse grows stronger…more frequent…The app isn’t just working…it’s reacting to something unseen — right there with them in that dusty silence.

While they gazed at the screen, fascinated by the pulsating light, it got colder. This change was strange and scary but also amazing. They were about to demonstrate that their device could not only detect but also interact with spirits.

Timmy took out his phone and said “We should record everything if we’re going to try this,” barely loud enough for Melinda to hear.

Melinda turned slowly in a circle with her eyes locked on the screen’s pulse. It grew stronger and concentrated on a point just a few feet away. They crept closer, searching the darkness with their eyes for what lay beyond the app’s reach. As they neared, a stack of books on a nearby shelf trembled slightly, as if nudged by an invisible breeze.

The chapter closed huddled together around shaking books while their app proved itself worthwhile second by second. What had started out as a casual experiment had become an immediate experience of encounter that would fuel future expeditions into uncharted territory. Their minds sparked with new possibilities – they knew that there must be more – as the line between here and there wavered at its thinnest point ever so slightly. As the books rattled harder, all three of them stepped back instinctively, fear mixing with awe in their wide eyes. The faint vibrations had grown into an audible shuffle as several old volumes began inching forward row by row from deep within the shelves themselves, pushed along by unseen hands.

“Do you see this?” Timmy asked in a small voice filmed the scene on his phone. Melinda's app blinked faster now casting blue shadows across their faces.

Josh moved closer reaching out toward trembling books being always more daring than anyone else while he spoke “There is something definitely here” recoiling quickly touched close behind shiver running down spine due sudden burst cold air which blew through aisle making pages open books flutter wildly.

Melinda suppressed initial fears driven scientific curiosity came closer shelf. “App’s readings are going haywire this could be some kind of spectral hot spot” observed hands shaking a little but voice steady holding phone still.

Library groaned like living thing as if in answer to their breakthrough adding its own soundtrack heightened atmosphere around them while Timmy continued recording panning phone over room hoping catch any other anomalies that might appear on video.

With every step app's numbers got higher and pulled further into library jumbling them up more with each turn they took shelves following signals felt like knitting needles through miles yarn air getting colder softer ambient building sounds growing louder distinct whisper movement slight wooden creak rustling paper.

On their way to the back corner of the library, the friends finally saw what had been causing all the noise. There was a large book sitting open on one of the reading tables. Its pages were turning one by one as if it were being read by invisible fingers. The old book was bound in faded leather and decorated with gilded motifs that gave off a soft glowing light.

“This is amazing,” said Melinda, staring at the pages flipping before her eyes. The app on her phone’s screen blinked rapidly and steadily like a beating heart. “It’s like it’s alive.”

Josh put his hand out but hesitated before touching the cover of the ancient tome; there was an electric crackle in the air around them when he did so, and it seemed as if the room got darker – now only illuminated by the phone and book.

“What does it say?” Timmy asked, his voice barely carrying over the sound of pages turning.

Melinda hunched closer, squinting into the dimness. The writing was in some kind of old English or Elizabethan script; impossible to read at a glance, but she could make out words about “strange ceremonies” and “the other side” and “unknown beings”.

A heavy feeling settled over them as they started to comprehend what they had found. The realization hit them like a punch: this app wasn't just a toy for ghost stories anymore; it was an invitation into another world entirely — one that has never been seen or imagined by mankind before now – and we're standing right at its doorstep…

Chapter 3:
First Contact

Joshua, Melinda and Timmy moved on under the pale light of the library's old-fashioned lamps. The ghosts of their previous breakthroughs still haunted their minds. Armed with their new tool—the app that proved to be able to detect specters—they tread deeper into the dark depths of the library, a place brimming with history and echoes from the past.

The ancient book they had found continued to flash sporadic beams of light, serving as a guide that led them further into their probe. The atmosphere around them hummed expectantly; it was as though the library itself was holding its breath and watching them closely.

As they made their way towards the rear of the building where the oldest and most neglected books were kept, the app began pulsing again. This time, it did so softly—almost in sync with the heartbeat of the library. Ever filming everything with his phone, Timmy had it out already, recording each second and every flicker on screen.

Melinda—who had quickly become unofficial leader for all things supernatural—told them to spread out; they needed more coverage. With her phone stretched before her like a divining rod, she directed them to a little-known corner of campus known for strange occurrences and inexplicable shivers among students.

There were rows upon rows here, packed tight with books that hadn't been touched since before any living student at this school could remember; titles embossed in gold long since faded away. The temperature dropped as they walked through those aisles—that unmistakable signifier of spectral activity now quantifiable through an app interface. Tightening shelves showed signs of dust having been displaced recently too – another common indicator something otherworldly might be near.

Out of nowhere, Melinda's phone shook violently in her palm—a sudden spike in activity that took even her by surprise. She stopped walking immediately—and signaled for Josh and Timmy who were still a few steps behind her to do the same. "Here," she whispered. "There's something here."

Josh and Timmy moved closer. The app indicated a presence directly in front of them. At first, they didn't see anything—just rows upon rows of old books and dust motes dancing in the flashlight beam. But then, slowly, a figure began to take shape in the air before the bookshelf.

It was faint at first – like smoke or a trick of light—but as they peered closer, it became more defined. A young woman appeared before their eyes, dressed in clothes from 1880s; her face serene but sad. She was see-through—ethereal—shimmering slightly as if made up not even mostly by particles but rather by motes that didn't know how to stop moving around each other.

The ghost didn’t seem to notice them at first; she seemed absorbed in what she was doing. Her hands were stretched out towards the books before her—they were slow and methodical; it looked like she was searching for something with one finger tracing over each title gently.

Melinda took a step toward her. “Hello?" she said softly—but loud enough so everyone could hear. “Can you hear us?"

The ghost stopped, her hands pausing on the back of an ancient book with a leather cover. She turned her head slowly to look at them, surprise flickering across her face as if she were not used to being seen. After a moment, she simply stared at them with deep knowing eyes and then nodded slightly before turning away again, fading slowly until she disappeared altogether, leaving only a faint cool breeze behind and the smell of old paper in the air.

Ecstatic from their encounter, they looked at each other in amazement. "Did you get that on video?" Melinda asked Timmy, who nodded with wide eyes behind the camera.

"Every second," he said incredulously.

Josh clapped his hands together excitedly, having forgotten all about his fear earlier. "This is it guys! It works! Our app really works!"

But instead of being satisfied by this peaceful encounter and allowing them to rest, curiosity surged through them like electricity after success had already been achieved in their first trial run. The library was just the beginning. "We should test it in more places," Josh said rapidly as ideas flew through his mind.

"Absolutely," Melinda agreed immediately as her scientific brain began processing all the data they had just gathered. "There are so many stories out there waiting for us."

With their device now validated by this friendly ghost sighting, they decided that they should explore other reportedly haunted locations both on and potentially off campus later down the line too. They leave the library feeling great and ready to delve further into what lies hidden within these shadowy depths of forgotten knowledge — but as soon as they stepped outside into cool night air everything changed around them; where once things seemed normal or boring now every inch hummed with unseen energy; each corner held secret yet-to-be-discovered histories… With every whispering wind there came another story — one which could be unlocked by an innovative new piece software such as theirs.

They put a big map of the school and the surrounding area on their table in the dorm room. Then they marked each haunted place with sticky notes. They had one triumphant star sticking out of the library where they'd made their first contact. They talked about each place in order, sharing stories and making guesses at what might be causing it.

Melinda grabbed her laptop, typing up all of their findings from that night into a new database. "We should track everything," she said. "Every little thing could be important; we need to record our methods, observations — even environmental conditions."

Josh was working on his phone app again. "I'm adding a log feature," he told them. "It'll automatically time-stamp and geo-locate any anomalies we detect, plus you can input notes right in the app."

Timmy watched footage of their library encounter scroll by on his camera screen. "This is good, really good — clear visual and visible readings on the app … this'll work great as research evidence."

Their planning session ran late into the night over cups of strong coffee and fueled by adrenaline from their discovery; they didn't want to stop talking now. It was agreed that they would begin expanded exploration next weekend — giving themselves more time for equipment refinement while also researching each location more thoroughly.

In this photo taken Jan 10, 2019, trio huddles around dorm room table illuminated by soft glow of Melinda's laptop. JOSH SPICER/FLICKR VIA CC BY-NC-SA

Chapter 4:
Gathering Shadows

The hype encompassing Josh, Melinda, and Timmy's ghost-tracking application rippled through the MIT campus as quickly as autumn leaves fell from its many oak trees. News of their initial success at the old library spread across dorm rooms and online forums alike, provoking a mixture of doubt and belief among students. Some brushed it off as an elaborate prank or coding trick, while others whispered about its implications in fearful fascination.

In the coffee shop where students gathered to study or relax between classes, the trio found themselves under constant surveillance. Conversations would halt when they entered, and some brave souls would approach them with questions or their own paranormal experiences.

"Can you really see ghosts with your app?" a freshman asked one day, her eyes wide with hope and skepticism.

Josh nodded eagerly; he loved any opportunity to show off what they'd accomplished. "More than see — detect. We're still working out the full range of it but it's real. We tested it."

Melinda was more reserved, her mind always on scientific logic. “We based it on actual technology we found that detects anomalies we believe to be spectral,” she explained matter-of-factly. “It’s not magic; it’s science.”

Timmy took a step back from the conversation and lifted his camera again to film his friends talking to someone so interested in their work. “We have footage. It’s not just stories. We’re documenting everything scientifically.”

With their growing fame — or infamy — came an increase in inexplicable events around them. At first it was subtle; books they needed for research would be left open in the library like they’d been anticipating which passages to reference all along. Lights flickered more frequently above their bathroom mirrors, and sometimes their electronics would freeze up with screens full of static before returning to normal.

One night as they were working on the app in their room, the air suddenly went cold. A tangible unease settled over them and their hair stood up on end. The app, left running on the table, began to emit a low, pulsing hum — an indication that something was nearby.

“Did anyone else feel that?” Melinda asked, pulling her jacket tighter around herself.

Josh looked around the room and nodded slowly. “Yeah. It’s never done that here.” His voice lacked its usual bravado now; it was cautious, curious.

Timmy picked his camera back up and turned it on, swiveling it around the room in an attempt to capture whatever the app had picked up. “There’s something here with us,” he said, mostly to himself. “Something... cold.”

The lens fogged up for a moment as if it had breathed in winter air too fast; when Timmy wiped it off on his sleeve, the shape of a person lingered in the condensation before vanishing again.

But this didn’t just happen to them. Other students who downloaded the app began reporting strange occurrences too: A music major practicing alone in an auditorium late at night felt invisible fingers press down alongside hers on the piano keys. A group of engineering students’ sensors went haywire outside old engineering hall at midnight.

Each story wove another thread in a tapestry of ghostly encounters that only grew more ominous with every new addition. The campus buzzed with an unseen energy — ancient and watchful.

The days got shorter and the nights longer, and so the three of them got deeper into the paranormal. But it wasn’t like before, they weren’t just trying to see things or make things happen anymore; now, Josh,

Melinda, and Timmy were part of something much larger. Before they came along.

Josh, Melinda, and Timmy stand beside the window in their dorm room as dusk falls over campus. Leaves rustle in the wind outside and long shadows stretch thin across everything until somewhere far off a dog howls—a sad sound that seems to fit with an atmosphere nobody can quite place their finger on. Behind them on the table sits the app, quiet except for one unnoticed flicker that suggests only more confusion is to come.

As soon as that eerie howl fades from earshot this room goes still in a way you can feel but not hear over the soft hum of equipment around them. All three keep watching out the window onto campus like a ghost might pop up among these autumn leaves.

What was once thrilling had become heavy: now there's weight behind every action. The adventure has shifted into reality where natural blends with supernatural without transition or warning. Earlier momentum still mingles with a current dread that has yet to be explained—neither fully understood nor gone away—only grown stronger since they started.

Melinda turns from the window back to look at the app on the table and picks it up again with its screen still flickering on and off in her hand "We need better documentation" she says this time steady when all else isn't "Keep track—log 'em see if there's any pattern or trigger."

Nodding Josh reaches for his laptop opens a new spreadsheet "Every anomaly we find"—he starts typing "Time place what happened environmental factors—we might get lucky enough for one of those to explain...or at least give context"

Hours fast forward through Timmy's camera until he sees a shadow nobody can explain with any of the natural light sources in the room "Look at this" he stops it points to the screen where there is a grainy image much darker than what should be behind it moving independent and separate "I didn't see this when I was filming."

And so they watch. The shadow plays its part on screen then just like that it's gone again. Room gets cold once more, heavier from before as if something else now knows they saw it.

"It's like. It's reacting to being observed." Melinda says through chattering teeth but mostly to herself "Or maybe we're just more sensitive to its presence now"

They decide they need more data for their experiment so they make plans to encourage other students to use the app too. Josh drafts a message to post on the student intranet:

"Have you experienced unusual phenomena with the Ghost Detector App? Please share your stories. Let's try and figure out what's going on around campus."

Soon after posting, replies were already coming in. While some were jokes of skepticism, others were honest descriptions of weird things happening; lights flashing in circuits that worked perfectly, temperature dropping for no reason, personal items moving when no one had touched them.

But one message stood out. It was from a grad student in physics who'd been using the app near the old particle accelerator lab. "The app went nuts," she wrote. "Then my papers — my decades' worth of research — they scattered like there was a windstorm at my desk. But I keep the windows closed tight and nothing else was moving."

Timmy swallowed hard, his voice brittle with nerves now. "This is getting beyond ghosts," he said. "It's like… disturbances in reality."

As they digested the reports rolling in, their understanding of the situation began to shift. They weren't just asking an app to detect ghosts anymore; they were dealing with an ability to interact with physical objects and environmental conditions; maybe with time.

The night wore on; the reports kept coming. The trio worked tirelessly, logging everything — every report of something strange or inexplicable — working through databases of local history and university records to cross-reference data points.

And though it was exhausting work that seemed never-ending, every entry cooperated into a larger picture of what appeared to be a much more intricate pattern than any of them had ever imagined.

The data consumed them: As they pulled deeper into it all, their dorm room became command central—papers strewn about like discarded dreams, laptops humming and glowing like so many sleepless eyes; the occasional soft pulse emanating from the phone app punctuating the only sounds left in tonight's quietude: friction between fingertips and screens; fingers cramping over keyboards and mice clicking at truth.

Their minds weren't made for this kind of work because nobody's mind is made for this kind of work because there shouldn't be such work to do. They should be studying for finals or going on awkward dates; not melting over probability densities or losing themselves in each other's eyes over correlation coefficients.

But none of that mattered anymore. They couldn't turn back now.

Not when they were so close to understanding what had happened — what they had done.

Josh leaned back, feeling his eyes ache. "We may have gone too far," he said, uncertain for the first time. "What if we are faced with something which is not only beyond our understanding but our control?"

Silent for a moment, Melinda thought hard before speaking again. Her voice was steady when she did finally say something. "We need an expert. Someone who has knowledge in not just technology but also…" She paused, searching for the word she wanted to use next. "…paranormal."

They decided to contact Professor Hammond, an anthropologist with a reputation for studying cultural beliefs about the supernatural. They wrote him an email early one morning about their project and what had happened so far, asking for any ideas he might have.

When they sent the message as faint daylight filled their crowded dorm room they all felt nervous and hopeful at once. Outside kids were headed to early classes and the world seemed almost normal again even though there were still strange things happening right next door.

Feeling refreshed by sunrise, they got back to work on the data. They sorted reports into categories: visual manifestations, physical disturbances, electronic interferences, psychological effects (the last of these being particularly unsettling – certain students had been having awful nightmares; others kept saying they felt like they were being watched; a few claimed hours would pass in minutes or vice versa).

While doing this it occurred to them that it wasn't just haunted places they were dealing with; it was haunted times as well. More things seemed to happen at night (especially around 3 AM) and under certain weather conditions – foggy mornings, stormy nights.

"We need controlled experiments," said Melinda, pulling up a calendar on her laptop screen. "We can't just collect data passively: we need to actively observe these events within controlled environments and try understand what's causing them."

Josh started typing up his plan while nodding along: "More cameras, more sensors…thermal imaging maybe…"

Timmy looked between his two friends and felt a swelling mixture of pride and fear. "And we need to be careful," he said quietly. "Because we're not dealing with code and theories any more…we're dealing with something else entirely."

As they prepared for the next phase of their project, their determination rekindled by daylight and shared belief in uncovering truth – They knew full well what was at stake; however, curiosity insisted on dragging them forward into the shadows which had gathered themselves around not only them but also within them.

Chapter 5:
The Alert

The morning was cool with a touch of autumn chill, which foreshadowed winter. The MIT campus was busy. Students were walking to and from classes, their breath visible in the cold air. It took Josh, Melinda, and Timmy past the old science building – red brick and ivy, offices of some of the most respected (and out-there) faculty members.

Professor Eldridge: retired physicist. Known for groundbreaking work in quantum mechanics – and more controversially – theories on where quantum fields intersect with paranormal phenomena. His office is located in the east wing of the building, a less-trafficked area where hallways are lined with portraits of scholars long gone, their eyes following students with equal parts curiosity and admonition.

His office door is slightly ajar; classical music seeps through it into the hallway—a violin concerto painting the air with melancholy. Melinda knocks gently on the frame of the open door.

"Come in, my young explorers." The voice comes from within —fragile yet still full-bodied.

Books and papers create a labyrinth within Professor Eldridge's office; there isn't a patch of wall that isn't shelved over and crammed full—physics bleeding into philosophy on every shelf. In the middle sits Eldridge himself – white-haired; lines dug deep like trenches across his face, but his eyes still shine like stars burning bright at eons' ends.

"We got your email," he starts as they make themselves comfortable amidst this ocean of knowledge. "You've caused quite a stir amongst my colleagues…" Playful tone underneath which seriousness soon surfaces.

Josh can barely contain his excitement about what they've found so far: "We think we've made headway in terms of detecting spectral phenomena."

Professor Eldridge raises one hand to pause him mid-sentence: "Yes yes… the app… clever piece of technology no doubt… But tell me, do you understand what you are truly meddling with?" His eyes dart across their faces; they feel fingers probing – searching.

Melinda responds with the calm confidence of a scientist: "…we're exploring new scientific territory—testing boundaries—"

“The boundaries…” Eldridge’s voice drops to a whisper. “The boundaries are there for a reason.” He leans back in his chair, fingers tented in front of him. “Science, my dear, is about understanding the laws of our universe. But there exist realms where those laws break down. Where science becomes … something else.”

Timmy speaks for the first time in minutes: “So are you saying we could be in danger?”

Eldridge nods slowly. “Exactly. When you open doors, sometimes you can’t control what comes through them. Some doors are closed for good reason—and once you’ve turned the key…”

The room gets colder; light dims imperceptibly – but just enough to make them shiver. Each syllable he utters seems to hang like a vapor.

Josh fidgets uncomfortably: “But we have precautions, methods to—”

“Precautions?” Eldridge chuckles—a sound that mocks their naivety. “Against forces you don’t even know? What precautions would you take against a storm you’ve never seen? A force of nature unknown?”

Looks were exchanged by the three. The professor’s metaphor hit them hard, but it did not shake their resolve to keep on going.

The determination in their eyes seemed to be visible to Professor Eldridge who then softened his gaze. "I know that you have what it takes and that your motives are pure. However, let me give you a word of caution; this is not just a path covered with mist of the unknown but beware of the dark you will invite."

As they left his office the meeting ended and those words echoed in their minds. The campus outside appeared less lively than before, shadows appearing longer.

Their eagerness was dampened by the weight of this warning as they walked back towards their lab. However, the unknown still called out to them – they couldn't resist it; there was too much excitement surrounding discovery at stake! Hence, funnily enough even though Melinda's heart sank fearing for what might happen next when dark things enter light places Timmy could see only questions waiting behind those shadowed doors…

With each step echoing through halls filled with echoes generated by scientific curiosity mixed with trepidation driven deeper into research undeterred by doom-laden conversation overheads ringing true while returning from visiting Eldridge Josh had been more worried about understanding why things go wrong than any other member present during our conversation

The proposal was met with approval and the next phase of their project began. They redistributed their duties with a renewed sense of purpose but also a new found sense of care. Melinda worked on improving the app's algorithm to include safety measures, possibly even a quick shutdown. Josh took it upon himself to upgrade their equipment; making sure everything was in its best condition and setting up additional cameras around their testing areas for wider coverage.

The day turned into night and the lab filled with the quiet hum of electronics and every now and then the click of a camera shutter. They worked together in silence, occasionally stopping to write something down or show each other what they had found. It felt like they were so close to something big, exciting, terrifying.

Finally breaking through the silence Melinda spoke up "We need to be methodical about this. If we're really opening doors like Eldridge said we need some sort of contingency plan. Something that safeguards us from... whatever may come through."

Josh paused his soldering to look up at her "Like an emergency containment protocol?" The idea seemed farfetched but then again so did most parts of this project.

"Yeah exactly." Melinda replied nodding “We’ll make it so we can cut off any occurrences quickly and safely if things get out.”

They moved onto talking about these new protocols. Timmy projected digital diagrams of the campus and surrounding areas on a screen, highlighting potential high-risk zones based off their data collection thus far. Melinda drew out initial ideas for containment protocols blending them into the app's interface as she went along. Josh continued fussing over hardware; trying to heighten its sensitivity while making it more reliable.

As night swallowed up the campus outside became alive with wind rustling through trees and against windows as if curious about what secrets were being revealed inside.

The trio carried on into later hours; their dedication contrasting starkly against darkening skies beyond the lab walls. They were no longer students or amateurs; they were pioneers teetering on the edge of an abyss, willing to confront what lay beyond armed with technology, courage and a growing sense of duty.

Amidst the flickering fluorescence of overhead lights, their work became a dance between trial, precision and error. Each member was wrapped in their own bubble of concentration surrounded by buzzing monitors and papers that rustled gently each time a draft crept through one too many under-sealed windows.

Melinda sat before her dual-monitor setup, code scrolling across screens occasionally halting to jot down equations in her dense neat handwriting. Her task was centered around embedding complex algorithms capable of remotely shutting down the app should it become uncontrollable or dangerous. To her each line was a barrier against some otherworldly force they could unwittingly unleash.

Josh had taken their theoretical designs and turned them into real tools with his practical skillset; he now busied himself assembling what looked like a satellite dish but with fail-safes that could disable it instantly if need be. Wire connected to solder wire connected to solder as his hands moved with well-practiced assurance, everything coming together exactly as planned.

On the other side of the room was a huge corkboard that Timmy had taken over. It was covered in maps, pictures, pages of hand-written notes — everything connected by strings that formed a web of theories and observations. He was meticulously going through each piece of visual evidence they'd gathered, putting timestamps on them, cross-referencing them against spikes in data recorded by the app. Each connection was a thread in the larger tapestry of their project; every note a clue to one of the mysteries they were facing.

The lab smelled like ozone and solder, an olfactory signature for all their technological efforts. Occasionally one or another would get up and stretch, having been getting stiff from sitting so long, then settle back into whatever task had become their rhythm.

Outside, the campus was quiet under night's blanket — but for every now and then when a late-night group walking nearby would let out a burst of laughter that cut through the silence. Those sounds seemed distant, otherworldly even; as if the lab were growing more insular, more absolute in its separation from whatever world lay beyond these walls.

Then suddenly there came a shift in atmospheric pressure; something electric filled the room with charge enough to make hair stand on end. Melinda's screens flickered — lines of code scrambled by static for half a breath too long before flowing normally again. Josh's soldering iron slipped from his fingers with a clatter as he jerked his hand back at once — it hadn't shocked him hard but there'd been some mild current sure enough tingling up his arm just now. Timmy's camera rotated itself around to face an empty corner of the room where there shouldn't have been anything worth watching.

"You guys feel that?" Timmy asked lowly as he came up to inspect the camera for signs of malfunction.

"Yeah," said Josh meanwhile checking his device for damage done. "This hasn't happened before, not like this."

Melinda got the app's data feed pulled up on her monitor quick as anything, her eyes running down the graphs for any unusual spikes. "There's something here with us. Right now," she said breathlessly while pointing to a significant peak in the readings.

They gathered around her screen and watched as the data pulse- pulsed- seemed to pulsate at an irregular rhythm, as if something — or someone — was trying to communicate through the very tools they'd created. The air grew colder, and a soft whisper seemed to come from nowhere and everywhere all at once.

"This is what Eldridge warned us about," Melinda whispered without looking away from the screen.

"Yes, but it's also what we need to document," Josh said, his curiosity newly stoked by that shock he'd just received. "Keep everything running. Record everything."

Timmy nodded and adjusted the camera so that it could see both the group and the monitors. "We'll get whatever's happening on tape."

With that they returned to their tasks albeit with heightened alertness and a sharper eye for detail than before. The room had ceased being a lab; now it was a conduit, a meeting-place of science and of magic where every reading — every abnormality brought them closer to knowing (controlling?) these things which are so near us always yet eternally out of reach.

Chapter 6:
Strange Journey

Under a night sky that lacked the light of moon, three stood outside the old Whitmore Asylum. The building, which was represented only by its sagging profile against the weak beams of their flashlights, had long been abandoned and left to rot. Among supernatural scholars in the area it was known as one of the most haunted places.

When Josh pushed open the asylum's gates — whose creaks and groans filled the air under a still night — a gust of wind swept through them like an exhale, as if the structure were breathing for what seemed like eternity for the first time in forever to welcome new visitors — but only those who already had one foot out of reality.

Melinda adjusted her backpack straps, which held their modified equipment with the latest version of their app for stronger spectral anomalies. "Remember, our task is to gather data not provoke any entity that may reside here," she reminded her team in barely more than a whisper.

Timmy nodded solemnly; his camera had been recording since they arrived at this entry point where he panned around to capture on film every detail within range — starting off with its spooky grandeur from outside crumbling walls pierced by dark unblinking eyes watching us move closer toward our doom while stepping on crunching gravel pathways during silent nights such as these until it grew larger before us. Then Timmy turned back toward Josh who stopped setting up additional sensors around base stations meant to extend app coverage but also boost sensitivity and awareness levels because according him "This should give us complete coverage over this whole place so we'll know if anything...significant happens;" spoken with equal parts fearfulness and eagerness.

In possession of prepared tools, they penetrated into deepest inside of asylum where main hallway swallowed all light leaving behind smell heavy with decay and everything forgotten years ago. Through darkness shone flashlight beams which caused shadows dance along peeling walls disturbingly.

With a quick swipe on her phone, Melinda activated the app. Immediately upon opening, many lights began to blink and change color on its screen. "Everyone! There's so much happening here!" She exclaimed with wide eyes locked onto what displayed in front of them. "These readings are way higher than anything recorded before."

They went further into building but but the more they proceeded air became denser as if sadness insanity once soaked these bricks still clung there forever melted into being structure itself. Camera picked it up — how light seemed like it was swallowed by darkness, sudden temperature drops, faint whispers that could barely be heard echoed through empty halls.

In former patient day room together they were frozen suddenly because chilling cold enveloped them whole and app let out shrill cry when shadows started taking shape at corners across from where they stood distortions of mankind writhing twisting around each other with sinister intention which couldn't belong anywhere except someplace else entirely evil.

Josh moved his shaking hand toward his backpack slowly then pulled out modified EMF reader while saying "We have to see if this is real or just... echoes", His confidence had been shattered away by what happened few seconds ago..

It was super cold by the time he got to one of those figures. It was also very windy when a strong force knocked the device from his hand, making it slide on the floor. The movements of the dark figures were aggressive and unpredictable.

"This is bad," said Melinda through gritted teeth. She clutch her brother Josh and Timmy, who was scared out of his wits. "We have to go now!"

They quickly went back while the ghosts came closer with loud eerie screams that were not just heard but felt in their chests, a deep painful cry of sadness and rage.

The closer they got to the exit, the more powerful everything became; even the walls seemed to vibrate with a wicked energy. Timmy looked behind him as they ran towards outside so he could film it for their channel but he tripped when the ground shook under them.

When they ran out into open space again, it was like trying to free themselves from an iron grip. But once they burst through those doors into night air, it suddenly felt so warm compared with how icy inside had been. They stopped for a moment once outside because their bodies couldn't take anymore and listened – faint screams still echoed off buildings around them, reminding what happened there.

After stepping out from under that heavy weight of an asylum atmosphere, something seemed to stick onto their clothes; something blacker than black itself. Their breaths came in ragged gasps which tasted of dust mixed with rotting meat each time they exhaled or inhaled again - it didn't matter which way you looked at this place really! It also felt like all life had been sucked out of world behind them as building slammed shut its mouth where no words could get past evermore so long as anyone knew better save herself unto thee...

Joshua Smith (aka Josh), Melinda Chenoweth (aka Mindy), Timothy Neeley (aka Tim) stood on cracked steps leading up away from old mental hospital. They could be seen against weak moonlight which finally penetrated darkened skies after what felt like eternity; though most would say that night had only just begun if asked when such light show started taking place over town. Looking back at towering structure with windows blackened & unwelcoming but still watching everything unfold below them - scared out of their minds! These three were professional ghost hunters who had never encountered anything quite like this before tonight.

When they got to the iron gates, which she had left open as they entered, Melinda checked her phone. The app was still running and it showed a rapid decline in spectral activity as they moved away from the building, but the readings were still abnormally high compared to any of their other investigations. “Look at this,” she said and turned the screen toward Josh and Timmy, her finger tracing the peaks of the graphs. “The activity spiked like crazy right as we were leaving. It’s almost like something wanted to keep us there — or make sure we never came back.”

“Could it have followed us?” Timmy asked, eyes darting over his shoulder at the darkness that seemed to breathe behind them.

“We need to go over the footage and data with a fine-tooth comb,” said Josh, trying to regain some semblance of his usual confidence. “Figure out what we’re dealing with. Might be worth getting

Professor Eldridge involved again, or finding someone else who knows more about this shit."

They paused at the gate for a moment longer before turning back toward campus, loading their gear into the car with slow deliberation born of exhaustion and adrenaline crash. The drive was quiet; gravel crunched beneath their tires while an owl called hauntingly somewhere in the distance. With each passing minute, hour or mile — there was no telling how long it took — what they had encountered settled deeper into their bones: not just as a scientific anomaly or intellectual curiosity but as a thing of real danger, an ancient anger awakened by their intrusion.

As soon as they left that place behind them for good — so they thought — would become clear only much later: Their journey into things beyond was far from over.

The car's headlights cut through thick curtains of night as they wound along narrow roads back toward campus: one vehicle on a deserted route stretching ever forward. Each bend felt like being dragged kicking and screaming from the clutches of the asylum, and indeed they had to pass under the sign bearing its name one final time. Shadows cast by trees lining the route flickered like the tail end of a bad dream, and though they recognized each landmark — a turn here; speed bump there — it all seemed infused somehow with some spectral residue left in their wake.

Inside, silence hung heavy as each tried to make sense of what had happened. Timmy replayed footage on his camera's small screen, fingers still trembling: shaky images etching his memory deeper. The ghostly figures grew more distinct with every review; hands outstretched as if trying to pull themselves free from recorded history into present flesh.

Melinda scrolled through readings collected on her app, scientific mind scrambling for explanations: brow furrowing with each graph analyzed; timestamps noted that correlated far too closely with most terrifying moments of their visit. "Energy levels spike every time there was a manifestation," she murmured half to herself. "There's a direct correlation … We provoked something with our presence … Something powerful."

Josh kept glancing in the rear-view mirror as he drove with one hand. He was gripping the steering wheel tighter than usual, half-expecting to see something other than the road behind them. "We need a new strategy if we're going to figure this out," he said finally, breaking the silence. "This isn't just about collecting data anymore. We need to understand what we're dealing with."

The interior light of the car was dim and flickering, casting eerie shadows across their faces and accentuating the gravity of their discussion. They debated whether they should return to the asylum — with better preparation, maybe more expert advice — or if they should focus on analyzing the extensive evidence they'd already collected.

The first signs of dawn began to touch the sky as they approached the city limits; the darkness slowly receded before the promise of morning. The light offered a semblance of normalcy, but it was superficial; pulling into campus, seeing buildings materialize from dim outlines into solid forms was a mundane sight that couldn't have been more different from everything that happened after dark.

"We should review everything first thing in the morning," suggested Melinda, her voice steady despite being weighed down by fatigue. "Go through all our footage, app data, notes; see if there's anything we missed in the heat of things."

"Yeah," agreed Timmy, clutching his camera like a lifeline. "I'll set up in the lab; we can project it all on big screen so we don't miss anything."

Josh turned off his car and pulled out his keys deliberately. "And I'll reach out to some contacts," he said. "Maybe someone else has dealt with something like this before. We could use all help we can get."

They unloaded their equipment – each piece a reminder of terror but also a tool for understanding – and walked towards their lab under waking sunlight that warmed their backs: a gentle assurance that daylight world was still there, still real.

As they enter the lab – sanctuary of science and light – ready to dissect their experiences under harsh and forgiving illumination of day. Each step back into the lab is a step away from darkness, but the shadow of night lingers: silent acknowledgment that their journey into supernatural was far from over.

Chapter 7: Unraveling

The three of them had set up their lab in a room on campus. Computers hummed, and the smell of solder and old coffee hung in the air. It had become a very tense place.

Timmy was pacing back and forth, watching the footage they'd captured play out on the big screen. Every time he saw it again, more color drained from his face. He was terrified. "We need to think about what we're doing here," he said finally, pausing it on a frame where a shadowy figure loomed out of the dark — or at least seemed to. "This isn't just some game or school project. That night at the asylum — it could have turned out so much worse."

Josh was calibrating a new sensor; he didn't look up when he spoke. "That's exactly why we have to keep going," he said flatly. There wasn't any fear in his voice at all; only conviction. "Nobody else has ever documented anything like this before, and we want to know what it is anyway? We're pioneers, Timmy."

Melinda was sitting in front of her workstation with thousands of lines of code open across multiple screens, spectral data graphs scrolling past too quickly for anyone else to read them; she looked over at him when Josh finished speaking and nodded along with him, thoughtfully adding: "I mean think about it — this could literally change everything we know about these kinds of experiences." She glanced down at one screen showing an analysis running but didn't really see it because she was already thinking three steps ahead to something else entirely: "The risks are nontrivial but so is any groundbreaking research."

He stopped pacing then and faced them both, hands raised as if gesturing toward everything around them: "But what if this goes wrong? We barely made it back last time!" His voice cracked on that last word, betraying just how close he'd come to not making it back at all.

Melinda sighed and swiveled in her chair to face him full-on; she looked at Josh because this was important but also made sure Timmy knew she meant every word of it. "We'll be more careful next time." Then she glanced down at her screens again, half-smiling. "I'm already working on a rapid containment or shutdown process for if things get out of hand again."

Josh set his tools down and came over to stand with them as he spoke: "And we won't go back there yet. We'll focus on controlled environments — smaller scale tests. Use what we've learned so far to fine-tune the app until we can handle whatever comes at us."

The room fell silent as Timmy stared at them both, considering their words. Finally he nodded, reluctantly: "Fine. But I mean it about the safety measures." Then he crossed his arms over his chest and looked from Melinda to Josh and back again: "And if anything even seems like it's starting to go wrong…" He let that hang in the air between them for a moment before finally sighing heavily and saying, simply, "…Agreed?"

"Agreed," said Melinda almost immediately, smiling a little wider now than before; Josh mirrored her agreement a moment later with something like relief flashing across his face right after hers had done the same.

With that decision made they got back to work pretty quickly after; Timmy went back to the editing station where he was logging every supernatural occurrence shown by their videos for later analysis while Melinda refined her code even more with layers of safeguards that could protect against any (or most) foreseeable future encounters — then Josh took charge on improving physical equipment durability around detection devices while reinforcing their ability too.

The day wore on faster than any of them realized it could; the lab was alive with energy and activity. Data streamed across screens in hypnotic waves, tools clattered softly on the workbenches, keyboards clicked under swift fingers. Outside, people were going about their business as if nothing out of the ordinary was happening — which, for them, it wasn't.

As the sun sets, sending dark shadows through the laboratory and a feeling of apprehension through the team, it is clear that they were wrong. The weight of their creation, for all they said and knew to be true about it, was oppressive in its stillness; it was watching them.

They grew closer with every test they ran. They drew closer to an understanding of a truth they didn't know existed until now. With each step forward, the less control they had over what was happening around them.

The evening deepened outside the lab's windows while inside it turned a darker shade, heavier with purpose. Somewhere between oscilloscopes and laptops, among stacks of books on electromagnetic theory and digital recorders that never really worked right anyway – somewhere there lay dedication.

Melinda code dived as night fell on her test machine at her desk cube farm farmville within a warehouse within an office park where everyone parked their cars because there was nowhere else to go so they drove around town aimlessly for hours after work before coming back here late into the night when nobody else would be around nobody ever came here never saw us no one cares we can do whatever we want everything is forgotten everything slips away what happens next will change nothing matters anymore everything is lost but not forgotten she stared at her screen surrounded by lines of code like snowflakes in a blizzard working through loops that twisted into themselves some days she thought she could almost hear them talking to each other speaking louder as she tried harder leaning back rubbing eyes palms temples letting slip loose hair down behind head neck spine feeling tense hot tired balled up clenched tight

Josh built things across from Melinda but only sometimes sat next to her when he wanted someone nearby whose presence wouldn't bother him normally maybe most times most likely probably not though sometimes always never too often enough he would lean over ask see this pointing at something on his screen could mean anything or nothing always never too often enough he would lean back say this won't work nothing ever does always never too often enough these things don't work that's why they call it the phantom cage is what he told everyone nobody else understood but they nodded so he kept saying it anyway nonetheless nevertheless all the same still yes

Timmy sat farthest away from anyone else, where no one could see him. On his computer was a camera feed showing everything happening in the room and another monitor with lines of code scrolling down it but neither mattered to him right now maybe most times most likely probably not though sometimes always never too often enough as long as there were tapes scattered around scribbled notes on hard drives and an old book open somewhere nearby he would be happy safe comfortable content relaxed at peace calm quiet dark alone with company distant still tense hot tight balled clenched tired hot cold sweaty wet

"Come on, let's see if we can manifest control using the data we have," said Josh, while anxiety still crawled under his skin. Melinda nodded, her fingers poised over the keys ready to shut everything down.

Timmy focused his camera to record things as they happened: both the experiment and their reactions which would become a documentary record of either a ground-breaking discovery or reckless stupidity—only time would tell.

Josh turned on the device and a low hum filled the room; the air became electric. The screens flickered; graphs spiked as the atmosphere in the lab shifted. Lights dimmed for a moment as power was diverted to the Phantom Cage.

"Anything?" asked Josh, peering at the monitors which now displayed an intricate series of data.

"Just small changes so far," replied Melinda, eyes scanning outputs. "Wait. There it is."

The center of the Phantom Cage seemed to ripple—visually distort—causing them all to take a step back instinctively. A shape began forming; at first vague and blurry, but becoming more defined—a shadowy figure with indistinct edges yet unquestionably human in form.

They watched with awe and fear as this apparition appeared before them—the most direct interaction achieved within this controlled environment experiment that represented their moment of truth about how far science could go or not go according to its own rules; but also what they were willing do themselves given their knowledge had been changed forever by what happened here tonight? The laboratory being now opened up like never before into another world altogether where understanding doesn't apply anymore once you realize there are other worlds around us too which we are part of through these kinds of experiments such as these ones happening tonight when all three witnesses saw different things from each other even though they were looking at same thing?

And as this humanoid figure once again materialized inside Phantom Cage itself then moved about within confines slowly taking on more substance than before like its body fighting against something invisible within us all – only this time it clearly struggled as if aware that we could see it too unlike previous occasions when such entities had simply ignored us completely while still remaining visible themselves somewhere else entirely within same space where we were standing right now so close together and Yet so far apart?

Around the Phantom Cage, the air started to get colder. It was a cold that you could feel in your bones and which made the breath visible as misty puffs. The lights in the lab dimmed even further until they were just computer screens glows and the eerie light from the containment field.

All of a sudden, it stopped moving and seemed to look right at them even though it didn't have any eyes or anything. The feeling of sadness was so deep and old that it almost filled up the room. Melinda felt a lump come into her throat and her scientific detachment crumbled under its weight.

"It’s... it's so sad," she whispered, barely letting out any sound. "Can you tell?"

Josh nodded silently, his usual bravado nowhere to be found. "Yeah. Like it’s lost or something, can’t find its way back." He looked over at the monitors where he saw that spectral readings were going off the charts. "This is real interaction," he said.

While they watched, slowly what could be considered an arm raised itself on the figure's part and reached out towards where they had set up their containment field boundary. It did so very slowly with purposefulness like this gesture was for them specifically. Timmy zoomed in on that moment with his camera recording everything at high definition; 4k resolution even capturing ghost hands pushing against invisible walls.

Melinda stepped forward suddenly – all her researcher instincts warring against an urge awakened newly within her for helping this trapped being – “I’m going to try communicate,” she said opening a program designed by herself direct communication between living forms nonliving specters alike “Let see if gets us.”

Josh didn’t stop but kept hand poised over shutdown button nevertheless warned low voice: “Careful”.

As Melinda types into her interface simple phrase ‘Can you understand us?’ words transform electromagnetic pulse pattern meant to interact spectral frequencies; and they wait in silence lab hardly breathing hoping for any sign of recognition at all from opposite ends that their technological bridge might stretch worlds apart.

Chapter 8:
The Ghostly Threats

The lab that used to be their dormitory was a planned and predictable space with dark corners that produced tension and strange happenings. As they delved further into the spectral realm, the three friends found themselves up against forces they could barely comprehend, much less control.

One stormy night, late as it was, the thunder crashing outside and rain tapping on the window pane, something in the air of their laboratory changed. They were running tests with the Phantom Cage — now permanently haunting one corner of the room — when this happened.

Melinda sat at her laptop adjusting settings, trying to optimize containment field stability. So absorbed she didn't notice at first when temperature in the room dropped. But soon enough she felt it: The cold that heralded spectral activity had never been so intense.

Josh watched environmental sensors from across the room. Then he began to watch them more closely. He didn't like what he saw. "Temperature's dropping fast," he said urgently, looking up from his screen as if to drive his point home with eye contact. "Way beyond normal spectral activity levels."

Timmy held his camera steady among fluctuating readings and an atmosphere heavy with danger. Fear tingled through his hands more than just from cold; he worried they might be outmatched.

As Melinda typed faster and faster, working her way through new algorithms to strengthen containment fields — she had started bleeding not long before Timmy's lamp shattered — a sharp pain cut across her forearm. She gasped and fell backward off her chair; her laptop clattered onto table over which it had once presided. A thin line of blood rose up along a deep scratch that hadn’t existed seconds earlier.

“Melinda!” Josh exclaimed and hurried to find first aid supplies.

“It scratched me…” Melinda murmured numbly, staring at her arm as if it belonged to someone else’s body. The wound was clean and precise, like a surgeon’s cut.

Timmy pointed his camera at Melinda’s arm, documenting the injury. His face had gone quite pale. “This is bad, guys,” he said quietly. “We’ve never had physical contact before; it’s getting more aggressive.”

Lights flickered ominously and growls vibrated through walls or floors or lungs — no one could tell which. The air seemed to thicken around them with electric charge, the moment before lightning strikes, when you know something has to give but have no idea what it will be.

“We need to shut everything down,” Josh said, moving toward main power controls. “Now. Before it gets worse.”

But when he reached for the switch, the room went black: No light except from Timmy’s camera blinking red and laptop screen still glowing grayish blue against dark wall in front of shocked friends who now could barely see each other save for occasional lightning flash that revealed them white as bones in briefest relief against their surroundings so clearly illuminated for just those few moments

During those flashes of illumination, they watched the shades travel.

around the Phantom Cage like they were being stirred by their panic. The breath felt wicked, as if one could touch it and know, that there was nothing around them anymore but themselves after having opened a door which cannot be closed.

Melinda held her hurt arm tightly and spoke with a trembling voice born out of determination amidst the stillness. "We gotta finish shutting it down or else if we keep leaving it on, it may become stronger."

Josh tried once more to find his way through power controls lit intermittently by lightning while Timmy recorded every second of their terrifying encounter with swirling patches of darkness.

They fight to regain control over their environment and experiment. Every flash reveals a different chaotic scene made worse by the fact that each is more terrifying than the last; such recurring events emphasize how much time is left for them. With Melinda injured and the events escalating, they are forced to confront not only physical hazards but also ethical limits surrounding what should have been done in researches.

The tension inside their makeshift lab seemed alive; it was tangible – hanging heavy in air alongside electrical charges brought about by storm beyond any windowsill ever built yet both were invisible since this room had none at all. Lightning would rip across sky making everything momentarily visible from within— three terrified faces staring back into space around humming Phantom Cage where shadows danced with scattered equipment amidst chaos littered here there everywhere atop tables covered desks floors walls strewn loose papers flipping wildly overhead like birds' wings flapping against wind.

Finally Josh made it to power controls where he reached out for emergency cutoff switch using his fingers seeking purchase. He grabbed hold of cold metal before pressing button firmly so that shutdown begins now without further delay. Then came winding down sound starting off high pitched whine gradually decreasing in frequency until swallowed up completely by howling storm ambiences.

However momentary sigh of relief fled away once mechanical noise faded and new one crept in. It was deep, resonant moan that seemed to come through walls from farthest reaches of building itself as if it were alive or something! A lamentation spectral – sounding like sorrow mixed with rage all rolled into one long drawn-out groaning which sent shivers down every spine present there.

Melinda, using table as prop against which she rested herself while applying pressure over self-made bandage on her arm, took in shallow breaths and thought quickly about their predicament vis-a-vis scientific knowledge coupled with sheer terror at hand. "It isn't just reacting towards equipment," she wheezed softly amidst moans so faint they could hardly be heard over said noise. "But towards us... our actions too; now we are part of this thing."

Timmy still kept filming events unfolding before him but his usually steady hands shook not only because he felt coldness biting through his skin but also due to realization that these were phenomena being recorded whose comprehension might defy not only their own but control mechanisms too.

Room felt electrically charged; hairs on bodies stood up straight due to static electricity. Shadows did not recede after Phantom Cage had been shut down; instead they pulsed independently with a life of its own. Another bolt of lightning struck and then grotesque figures cast themselves upon walls—shapes twisted around corners where shadows should have stayed still forevermore if only there wasn't any movement behind them at all

"Light, more light," Josh yelled, reaching into the blackness for a flashlight. He found one on a shelf beside him and with a click, he sent a beam of light slashing across the room.

The shadows seemed to scatter before it; they retreated into corners and under things. They were only reprieved enough to see where they were. Melinda used the light to get a better look at her wound; it was worse than she'd thought and blood was coming through the makeshift bandage.

"We need to get out of here," said Timmy urgently. "Whatever we've done, it's not safe down here. We can't just turn this off like a piece of equipment."

Josh nodded grimly. "Back to main building. We need medical supplies for Melinda, and we have to figure out what the hell we're going to do about this."

They gathered everything they needed -- Melinda's laptop, Timmy's camera which was still recording somewhere upstairs in the dark, any hard drives that had their data on them -- and made another cautious approach to the door.

As soon as they exited, a gust of wind slammed the door shut behind them with a bang that echoed down the hallway. They stopped dead in their tracks and listened: nothing but rain beating against windows outside.

Moving through dark empty corridors of dorm building with each shadow potentially dangerous each noise alarming retreat is tense hurried driven by overwhelming need to escape from lab room As storm outside rages matching their turmoil provides perfect backdrop for terrifying events of night As they exit cool air hits them contrasting sharply with stifling fear left behind

They found the main building, luckily it was open. Inside it was like another world. The warmth hit first—the welcome release from the icy hands of the storm. Fluorescent lights buzzed overhead, casting even illumination which was a far cry from their lab with its flickering shadows.

They leaned against the wall once inside, catching their breaths. Water dripped off them and pooled at their feet and Melinda winced at readjusting her grip on her arm. “I need to see a doctor,” she said through gritted teeth. “This looks bad.”

“We’ll hit up the campus clinic first thing,” said Josh, checking his watch. “Late as it is, someone should be on call.”

Timmy switched off his camera and looked around the empty hallway. “Do you think it followed us here?” he asked quietly.

Josh shook his head, though there wasn’t much confidence in his eyes. “No, I don’t think so. These things are location-bound, or so we’ve gathered. We’re safe here.”

Melinda wasn't convinced. "We don't know enough about what we're dealing with," she said grimly. "It's not behaving like anything we've read about. This isn't just residual hauntings; it's intelligent, reactive."

They agreed to stay in the main building for the night—there was no way they were going back out into that storm or near the lab until morning—and Josh found some blankets in a storage closet while Timmy scouted for threats and Melinda tried not to pass out from pain in an alcove beside him.

Adrenaline had carried them this far but now that they were safe, exhausted and deeper fears began clawing their way back up through their spines: What had they done? Was this all for nothing?

They were sitting together in a dimly lit classroom down one flight of stairs from the main floor, where the ambient light from the hallway outside seeped in through a narrow window in the door. The storm was screaming and throwing itself against the glass and they couldn't have felt more alone. They had been talking for hours about what to do next—how to contain it, how to reverse it if they could—but now their words were running out. Each noise from outside was a finger pointing at them from beyond what they knew.

It got later and later. The storm's fury seemed to be matched only by the chaos wrecked upon Timmy's insides. He had been silent since they left the lab, but now his eyes kept flickering up towards the windows where rain was leaving ragged streaks down the glass and each rumble of thunder sent another wave of dread sloshing through his guts—the ghostly entity he knew should have been contained within lab walls but wasn't

Melinda's arm hurt. She sat, staring into space, thinking. Everything she'd ever learned about the scientific method ran through her mind at once. Every bit of data, every encounter — something had to tie it all together or at least give them a starting point for defense. "We have to start over," she said, more to herself than anyone else in the room. "Every test, every variable. We must've missed something that tells us how to contain it."

Josh kept pretending like he was in charge, but the dark corners of the lab seemed to get closer with each passing hour and every input they made on their phones reminded him how scared he was getting. The list went something like this: professors; paranormal experts; anyone who might be able to help them figure out what they were dealing with and how to stop it from doing whatever it wanted in there any longer than necessary. "We're not alone," he assured his friends without much inflection behind his voice this time. "Other people have dealt with things like this before. We'll find somebody who can help."

Then came ideas for what they could do once help arrived — which only made everything sound more hopeless. They talked about lining the perimeter of the lab with salt; Melinda thought that might be bullshit since this thing didn't seem bound by traditional understandings of What Paranormal Stuff Is And Isn't Capable Of.

“Maybe we could try a digital exorcism?” Timmy suggested half-seriously through gritted teeth, looking as if he’d worn out one too many jokes lately on subjects surrounding their current predicament.

“Like… if it’s interacting with our equipment,” he continued more seriously now, trying to keep his voice steady while still showing how panicked he was over all this, “then maybe we can drive it out electronically?”

Melinda’s brain started ticking again at that thought — Timmy’s idea having been just absurd enough to be worth entertaining. “That’s actually not the worst thing I’ve heard all night,” she said, slowly. “What if we inverted the field generator’s polarity and created, I don’t know… some kind of electromagnetic repulsion field?”

For a while, they kept talking about things that only required them to know what they were talking about — but eventually the rain stopped and dawn started hinting at itself through the watercolor gray of morning painted across those old windows, and they knew it was just about time to go back inside.

They knew their next move could kill them. And also:

But with every bag zipped up tight and each footstep towards safety growing further away, something else took hold of them. The storm had passed outside; light had begun sneaking back into the sky; whatever that thing was waiting for them down there in that lab didn’t stand a chance.

So they walked out of that classroom armed with science and an even stronger desire to figure out what exactly happened last night — no matter how much it terrified them.

Chapter 9:
Gone Round The Bend

Josh, Melinda, and Timmy have never known this kind of thing. It used to be that their experiments were conducted in labs or haunted houses, but now the paranormal keeps following them everywhere they go. This intrusion into their personal spaces has been relentless.

Josh's Apartment:

Josh had always taken pride in his apartment as a retreat from work and school—now it seemed he couldn't even escape there. Things would move around; books would fall off shelves when no one was near them; he'd find his glasses in the bathroom when he knew he'd left them on his bedside table. Once, he woke up to the smell of gardenias—he could picture exactly where that would have come from. Gardenias were his grandmother's favorite flower; they meant lazy Sunday afternoons and home-cooked meals and little boys hiding behind their mother's skirts while their fathers watched football games on TV. At first Josh thought maybe it was just that—forgetfulness, overwork. But one night he woke up to whispers in the living room.

He got out of bed slowly, listening hard before pushing open the door to investigate what sounded like an argument between two people trying not to wake anybody else up. He looked all through both rooms but found nothing, just an electric silence that made his skin buzz.

Melinda's Studio:

Melinda's nightmares are more visual than auditory: shadows morphing into shapes across walls and ceilings—a man with long arms standing by her bed at night—and when she wakes up it takes her eyes several seconds to adjust back to reality because everything is so much darker than she remembers leaving it.

Her scientific equipment is always scattered across the floor every morning—anomalies with explanation—but once she saw her computer screen flicker on while she was sleeping beside it and spit out pages of code she didn't recognize, cursor moving as if responding to a touchpad in another room. Sometimes she wakes up thinking there's been a power surge because all the numbers on her digital clock are different, but they're always hours ahead or behind where they should be, and for a few seconds after waking she can never remember what time it is.

Timmy's Dorm Room:

The audio recorder Timmy uses to capture environmental sounds during their investigations has become a medium for mysterious vocal phenomena. When he plays back recordings meant to document the ambient noise of his own dorm room, he hears low murmuring voices under the static—words whispered too quickly and too quietly to understand, but with an inflection that must mean something: urgent, begging, sometimes angry.

The voices get louder every night; Timmy doesn't know if it's just him or if his roommate can hear them too—he hasn't asked—but he has trouble sleeping because he knows they want something.

The psychological cost of this new level of exposure takes a heavy toll on all three of them. They stop sleeping properly: when they do manage to drift off, they dream about themselves dreaming in their dreams—a house of mirrors that stretches out into infinity.

Their group meetings become as much about sharing notes on their hauntings as sharing research—they compare symptoms more than solutions—and around campus there are rumors that the laboratory is cursed.

After yet another day filled with personal hauntings (the worst yet), Timmy finally breaks down one evening when they've gathered in Josh's living room with all the lights turned off. The only illumination comes from a single lamp beside the couch—it makes everyone look sickly.

"We can't keep going like this," he says—his voice is hoarse from lack of sleep—and neither Josh nor Melinda disagrees; both nod their heads vaguely towards him without making eye contact. "Whatever we've started isn't bound by walls or objects—it's attached itself to us."

Melinda, her eyes black with tiredness, nodded. "Understanding, controlling these things has been our study ever since. But we are not in control of anything. It controls us."

Josh was staring at his grandmother's photograph on the mantel. He turned to them with what he felt was a determined look on his face and said: "Then we should take it head-on. Let it spread – let alone win the fight. We have to find a way of pushing it back or sealing it off."

As they strategized, pooling their collective knowledge to devise a plan. Each suggestion is debated fiercely, their desperation fueling a determination to reclaim their lives from the haunting. They decide to delve deeper into the research, to understand the nature of their attachment, and to sever it, whatever the cost. As they talk, the wind outside dies down, as if listening, waiting for their next move.

In Josh's dim living room, they laid out maps of all places investigated pinned with notes about types of phenomena experienced and strengths of manifestations; speaking softly so as not attract attention from unseen entities that surround them.

Melinda had her laptop open cross-referencing personal experiences against data collected from those sites looking for patterns or common denominators that could help solve this mystery: “There seems be a correlation with electrical disturbances recorded,” she pointed tracing lines numbers on screen “Every site including now our homes shows significant electromagnetic anomalies… It’s like we have become conductors through which energies embodied by such creature’s flow.”

Timmy stood beside her peering over shoulders added "And it's not just random noise either; there appears intent behind some bits though silent whispering voices keep coming up frequently whenever something moves close enough – but never quite clears out sight range before fading again”

Josh paused in pacing near fireplace thinking deeply while saying “Or maybe we’re part message," he suggested grimly "Maybe places aren’t what matters but ourselves. We got ourselves marked by curiosity – poking around where we don’t belong.”

The room was heavy with idea, a new and more personal threat. They were no longer just observers but had become part of the phenomenon itself. This realization brought a new level of fear but also a galvanized resolve.

“We need to isolate common factor,” Melinda said looking at their digital logs “Every experiment every location there must still be something missed.”

They divided tasks each person taking section of data collected to analyze further; living room became temporary headquarters filled with papers, books, and various electronic gadgets strewn across tables and chairs as they worked late into night

As they worked on isolating the common thread among all experiments conducted over past weeks which have led them this point where every place seems haunted (even these homes) . The more they looked through their notes taken from different locations visited during investigations done so far, the less everything made sense until Timmy shouted excitedly pointing audio file recorded at abandoned mill: "Guys listen carefully beneath statics you can hear it whispering."

They pressed nearer when he played the recording, the speaker crackling with static. But behind it, under it, beneath it all; if you didn’t know what you were hearing for you might never have heard it – was a quiet pounding, like a heart.

“That’s the noise I got on my recorder in my room,” said Timmy. His voice was strained. “It’s been there all along, like… beckoning.”

Melinda compared the sound to electromagnetic readings taken at the same time. “It matches up. This pulse — it appears at every major event, every key interaction. It’s like a signature.”

So they formed an idea: The things weren’t just reacting to them; they were woven together through this pulse, this spectral heartbeat that connects all the haunted places — and now them.

“We need to disrupt it,” said Josh through gritted teeth. “If we can break that cycle by stopping this pulse… maybe we’ll cut off whatever’s feeding on us.”

Creating something which could neutralize the spectral pulse without aggravating any of the phenomena would be dangerous.

While they conceived and built this device - working tirelessly into the night as their sleep became haunted by new visitors who grew steadily more intimate with them - they knew that each moment brought them closer to having worked for nothing but their own demise. Every instant in which these people sat still and tried to help only revealed another clue that they were running out of time before everything caught up with them: The shadows grew darker and heavier around those who had seen too much; sinister whispers filled their ears whenever silence fell too long or light dimmed too low; an oppressive sense of dread seemed to hang heavy in air around them, making it harder and harder just breathe let alone think clearly.

Chapter 10 : Loneliness

As they experienced more and more appearances of ghosts, not only in frequency but also in intensity, the three friends realized that they were losing touch with the world. Josh, Melinda and Timmy once enjoyed being part of a lively community at school, engaging with their peers and professors; however, driven by anxiety and curiosity about the supernatural, they became involved in research which gradually distanced them from others.

They began to withdraw from society almost without knowing it. Their friends noticed that they always looked disheveled and tired and that their conversations had become narrow-minded. Formerly interested in various academic fields, now all they talked about was haunted houses or poltergeists or data collected during paranormal investigations. Social invitations stopped coming altogether; if somebody managed to persuade them to show up somewhere outside of university premises – where they spent most of their days – it was clear that all three were preoccupied: checking ghost-hunting apps on phones or freaking out over some innocent sound.

Their university grades also suffered as a result of their obsession. Professors noticed Josh's, Melinda's and Timmy's decreasing attendance rate together with deteriorating quality of assignments submitted when handed in at all; before long educational records which used to shine so brightly got covered in dust too. Eventually even Professor Eldridge himself – who happened to be their thesis supervisor – had no choice but approach them after what seemed like eternity since any actual studying took place; instead there had been delivered sloppy presentation touching on quantum physics only because theory related somehow with parapsychology.

"You have developed this... one-track mind," he tried to explain his feelings but could not hide worry behind words, "and while I understand passion — your enthusiasm is admirable — you're missing out on rest world knowledge which we must absorb for sake future employability. This tunnel vision kills careers."

"Our work matters," replied normally composed Melinda bluntly, "you should know better than anyone else how serious things are."

It was an uncomfortable conversation that only deepened their sense of isolation.

Family relationships took a hit. Parents could hear stress through phone lines and worried why kids called so late or sounded different; "You don't sound yourself" used to be Josh's mom main question every other day, her voice trembling with concern, "everything okay? you sure don't want come back for little while?" Even Timmy's younger sister during rare visit home once said: "You look like you've seen ghost" without realizing how accurate description was.

And then their safe places became anything but. Their bedrooms became filled with screens and physics papers as they tried to figure out what was happening outside those doors; pages were tacked onto walls or strewn across floors like some post-apocalyptic Matisse landscape in which colour represented time travel theories, and words were thoughts interrupted by sleepless nights or another lukewarm cup of coffee brewed from machine working overtime because it didn't know any different.

The more they shut themselves off from everything except desperate attempts towards understanding – the only cure for these hauntings being knowledge itself – the less space remained between them and whatever lurked just beyond perception. There were studies which showed that people who spent too much time alone began going mad even if there had been nothing wrong initially; this made perfect sense when considered alongside fact that most days conversations with outsiders ended frustration since nobody else had clue about world outside own experiences.

They sit in lab one night, computers humming softly as they always do when phantom cage is active. Stacks upon stacks of articles surround them - each labeled neatly by topic, author name highlighted yellow marker pen - while empty mugs from vending machine stand like sentinels between piles which rise higher than ceiling tiles allow; hands hover over keyboards but never seem quite ready type anything new despite need for answers growing stronger with every hour. "We're alone now," says Josh finally after what seems like eternity, his voice flat against cold laboratory walls; we can't expect anyone to understand."

Melinda nodded her head, not taking her eyes off the screen that displayed numbers that were going up and down. "Then we will work it out ourselves. We have to."

Timmy lifted his camera with a determined look in his eye. "And we'll record everything. So when we get out of here, people will know what went on."

Everything outside of them had dropped away. They were just old things they used to be as they sank deeper into themselves and whatever had taken hold of them. Every test brought them closer or took them further.

The lab was dark, smelling like bad coffee and lightning storms, the silence between them suffocating in its heaviness. The most noise came from Melinda's typing every once in a while, or Josh muttering under his breath as he tried to fix sensors that didn't seem to be sensing anything anymore.

It looked less like a lab than a fort that was being attacked from all sides. There were formulas and diagrams tacked up next to photos of weird shapes or whatever it was they had seen floating around the room last week, which made their brains feel like scrambled eggs.

Cables crawled everywhere over the floors so you couldn't walk without tripping on something that could probably electrocute you if you weren't careful.

But outside this place everything was still normal for everyone else. The leaves turned colors because it was fall but it stayed hot in California anyway so they didn't feel any better about freezing all the time even though their bones felt brittle enough to shatter at any moment. And their friends kept walking by like they hadn't known each other since freshman year or seen each other naked at some point.

"Have you noticed how weird they've been acting? They look like ghosts," one girl said as she hurried past the door, which wasn't closed all the way because nobody had left for days.

Inside Timmy adjusted his camera so it could see not only the weird stuff but how bad they looked getting worse. It caught all their faces like it was supposed to do but it also caught the shadows that stayed even when there wasn't anything to cast them.

Melinda rubbed her eyes and then started typing again, collecting numbers from tests that didn't make any sense in a pile that kept growing. "We're missing something," she said, more to herself than anyone else as the screens blinked at her with nothing helpful. "There's got to be some kind of pattern we're not seeing."

Josh walked over and put his hand on her shoulder when he heard her say it from across the room. “We’ll find it,” he said in a voice that was tired but tried not to sound like it. “Whatever.”

But even though he meant for it to mean something, there was a thing behind his eyes that made you think maybe he felt different about what everything meant now, because after everything who’d still believe in miracles? So then he went back to his station without saying anything else because talking seemed like something you did for fun and this wasn’t fun at all anymore.

Their lives had also been bad on a personal level. Calls home had become less frequent and more forced. They were filled with half-lies and false reassurances – “Yes, mom, everything’s fine, just busy with the project,” Josh would say, deflecting her worried questions. “No need to worry.”

But worry was there: it slept beside them at night. Every strange noise in their apartments, every flicker of light – it all brought them back to the world they couldn’t escape. They slept fitfully and dreamed vividly, haunted by whispers that followed them into waking.

They convene on a stormy night; wind outside howls like the spectral voices that now fill their recordings. Gathered around a mass of equipment in the center of the lab, they begin another test – this one bigger, more dangerous than the last. The glow from the Phantom Cage paints their faces blue and hardens shadows that shift with each pulse of the machine.

“Ready?” Josh asks, looking from Melinda to Timmy who nod back; their expressions are stoic.

“Ready,” they say together — bracing for what they don’t know; alone but together still; haunted but not hopeless; driven by a flickering hope that maybe they can undo the dark thing they’ve done.

The storm rages harder outside and its symphony joins with our machines’ low hum until our lab is a surreal theater of shadows and light. Bathed in monitor glow and Phantom Cage luminescence we stand on this precipice none of us knew was coming when we signed up for grad school. Around us machines blink and screens flicker while wind howl mixes with ethereal whispers from recordings — seeps into every bone of this place.

Melinda initiates frequency pattern change in containment field hoping it disrupts spectral manifestation somewhere between here & there (how do you solve this equation?). The air in the lab gets thick with charge, like the building itself knows they’re about to break through. She squints at the data streams, watching for anomaly.

Josh watches the Phantom Cage – never too far from that emergency shutdown lever. It’s hard for him not to think about what they’re doing here; those boundaries are getting blurry. This is uncharted territory — where science maps end and folklore begins.

Timmy just keeps recording; his camera’s seen everything so far and it’ll see this through to the end. He twists a knob as lights within

Phantom Cage start oscillating; wild patterns dance across walls. They stand framed in his viewfinder against a backdrop of controlled chaos – tells you all you need to know about what's at stake here.

Without delay, equipment sparked and sent waves of energy throughout the laboratory. Monitors blinked on and off, and the air sizzled with electricity. A resonant tone filled the room—deep and vibrating, as though it came from everywhere at once. Melinda stared at her monitors in astonishment. "It's…" She hesitated to complete her thought.

Josh noted how shadows seemed to retract from the light spilling out of the cage, as if they were recoiling from their own unleashed power. "It's working!" he said, his voice half triumphant and half relieved. "Keep it going!"

But then something shifted. Success soured into a premonition of doom at the experiment's climax: The corners grew dark with impenetrable shadow; recording after recording emitted spirit voices climbing ever higher in pitch and volume until they threatened to drown out even the loudest mechanical hum.

Timmy panned his camera across their faces and saw reflected there an awful truth he wished he hadn't voiced aloud: Cold settled over him like damp cloth; frigid air blew in through unseen cracks in his courage. "Guys," he whispered hoarsely to his friends. "I think we need to shut it down."

Melinda—for whom data was oxygen, readings a pulsebeat—nodded reluctantly between quick breaths meant to steady her hands over buttons whose labels she couldn't see anymore: Shut … now … regroup … analyze …

Josh reached for the lever—and as soon as he pulled it down, all the lights went out with a flicker that left them clawing through sudden darkness back toward their own bodies' reflexes for survival time-tested before fire.

In this blackness there was only one source of light, one pulse still stubbornly glowing despite all deactivation efforts: Phantom Cage.

Their gloves not warm enough against cold metal surfaces, breath visible in cold lab air—they fumbled at backup power systems, each knowing that they had crossed over and entered a place from which there might never be easy entrance back. Light! Now! Safe!—but really they were chasing these for a different reason altogether: because only in their absence would the true cost of curiosity reveal itself to those who had paid most dearly for what they thought was knowledge but turned out to be loneliness.

Josh, took baby steps towards the back of the lab where the generator buzzed a low, steady hum, louder than the chaos would imply. He swept his flashlight over the area as he reached it—nothing wrong there. He checked the connections; his fingers were numb from cold that had gripped this room for hours now, unnatural cold coming from within rather than from autumn outside.

"All clear here!" he called back, more confident than he felt. "Everything's running but it's not getting to the main systems!"

Meanwhile Timmy kept rolling on his camera as they scrambled to troubleshoot. He moved over to document Melinda at her console, focus sharp enough to pick out each bead of sweat on her forehead even in this freezing air. His hands were steady—he'd learned long ago how to hold them rock-steady for moments like these—but his mind raced with what all this meant. Each frame was a record of their fall into a place where science met superstition; every clip could be a clue toward escape or death.

Melinda found it—a blown fuse at the main power console from that first surge. "Got it! Replacing now," she said, some relief creeping back into her voice as she worked.

She fit the new one in, and overhead lights blinked on before stabilizing with an indifferent hum. They flickered hesitantly for a moment before steadying themselves, bathing everything in harsh white light that pushed shadows into corners. The sudden brightness was blinding; they all blinked against it for a moment.

With light came safety but also tension: The air still prickled with leftover electricity and made their hair stand on end. The Phantom Cage kept pulsing—the light inside had dimmed somewhat but none of its menace had been lost.

"We gotta contain it," Josh said without taking his eyes off cage. "Whatever we let out isn't going back easy."

Melinda nodded briskly, running through options in her head. "Let's set up a controlled feedback loop. If we can't shut it down, maybe we can dampen its energy—make it more manageable."

Timmy swung the camera over to catch this new determination. "What do you want me to do?"

"Document everything," she said firmly. "We need a record."

As they rigged their last chance at reeling in these ghostly phenomena, cables were reconnected and settings adjusted and Timmy's camera rolled on for every single damn step. The storm had ended outside, but its calm was misleading—the lab still thrashed with one inside. As they activated the feedback loop, the air buzzed with electricity and the unknown: science's hum against paranormal throb, hoping for salvation if not survival.

Chapter 11:
The Hunt

Beneath the colorless light of a dying moon, the old Whitmore Asylum loomed like a monolith of emptiness in its writhing cloak of overgrown grounds. Its decayed outline spread long sinister shadows across them. Wind whispered through shattered panes and barred windows, carrying with it the chill of fall and the faintest hint of that place's dark past.

Three people moved toward it—Josh, Melinda, Timmy—ahead full determination mixed with dread. Their steps were heavy not only from their equipment—cameras, recording devices, Phantom Cage 5.0—but also from their need to prove this reality to an ignorant world.

"Get in, set up, record everything by morning," Josh said flatly; his hands shook when he adjusted his backpack. "No matter what happens we stick together and follow the plan."

Melinda nodded grimly and clutched her laptop bag which held all her data for tonight's work behind a mask of resolve. "I've programmed the app to alert us if there are any significant anomalies. We'll see any spectral activity in real-time."

Timmy panned his camera across the front of asylum testing focus on different angles capturing its presence eerily well. "This will be our most important footage ever" he said gravely indicating depth they were about step into.

The door swung open on rusted hinges as they approached main entrance allowing them step right into cold blast air that smelled stale mingled abandoned with night outside it was hard distinguish where one began ended. Inside their flashlights cut through darkness casting light peeling paint walls covered graffiti debris strewn across floor testament violence both distant recent have occurred here at hands curious brave alike.

Having set up base camp main hall Josh placed Phantom Cage 5.0 strategically so that sensors cover expansive area; Melinda set workstation linking data feeds various sensors placed throughout hall her laptop; Timmy positioned cameras different angles all corners were watched.

When they powered on their equipment the familiar hum filled air as light glowed but didn't come from any this world. Screens flickered graphs numbers scrolled across them showing environmental conditions being monitored.

"We're good to go. Everything's operational," Melinda said, eyes scanning real-time data. "Now we wait and watch."

Waiting was hardest part of these nights; minutes stretched into hours until eternity seemed to pass while they sat surrounded by oppressive silence. A floorboard creak or scatter debris jumbled nerves because each reminded them unseen could be very near—just out reach their lights' circles.

At some point after most of night already had withered away and moonlight itself began fade Timmy's camera picked up an anomaly: a slight distortion in air like heat shimmer but cold touch as Melinda pointed out when it passed her station.

"There!" he hissed swiveling focus this anomaly that moved around, "Do you see it?"

Something was definitely here, Melinda confirmed as she watched the electromagnetic readings on her screens spike. Her voice trembled with fear and excitement.

Josh focused on the Phantom Cage, ready to adjust its settings — either to contain or amplify the spectral presence. He ordered: "Keep the cameras rolling." His eyes never left the air, which seemed to shimmer and hum with a life they couldn't see.

The temperature in the room dropped as they recorded. The feeling that something big was about to happen became so strong it was nearly unbearable. But what had started out for them as a hunt had become something more: proof of a haunted world's truth before their very eyes.

The longer they stayed at Whitmore Asylum, the more pronounced and invasive the anomalies became. It would feel like the place was actually waking up around them — distant footsteps; hidden movements; figures appearing then vanishing — and by morning there would be no doubt in their minds that they'd crossed over into realms from which no one has ever returned unchanged.

The night weighed heavily on Timmy's mind when he set his cameras up around Whitmore Asylum. The building itself seemed hunched against him, full of secrets it refused to give up. So many terrible things had happened within these walls, and if there were any justice in this world or others, every last soul should have been allowed to rest in peace.

But instead their equipment hummed into this dreadful silence; cold floodlights washed away darkness but only revealed decay; thermal imaging showed empty rooms registering temperatures colder than ice.

Josh stood watch beside Melinda as she tapped keys and scanned data during one long midnight hour after another. When he wasn't pacing near her workstation, he trained his eyes on the Phantom Cage — specifically whatever odd pattern its readouts might produce while an entity powerful enough to care about such things prowled unseen through its domain.

Melinda surrounded herself with light: lines and dots on a dozen different screens that might add up to a tale of this place's past or present — if only she could crack their code. Now and then, though, her eyes would wander up to the thermal imaging feed. She wanted to see these ghosts, with their pockets of cold that roamed the halls. But even through two sets of circuits they were still invisible.

Timmy wanted his cameras — all 10 of them scattered throughout the building — to be his eyes and ears. More than just recording the physical changes in the environment around him, he hoped they'd capture what each member of the group was going through inside their own heads. He spent much of each hour panning from face to face: determination on Josh's; fear flickering behind Melinda's.

Then one moment everything changed. One moment it felt like Whitmore Asylum wasn't just a haunted house but a haunted soul — like Timmy was there not as an observer but as part of something deeply broken that desperately needed to heal itself.

It started with a groan. A low sound so long and mournful it seemed impossible for something human or mechanical to have made it — especially not here, especially not now. The three investigators stood frozen in place, watching each other for confirmation that they hadn't imagined what they'd just heard.

The sound held its pitch for several seconds before gradually fading away — but as it did so, something else happened: It echoed back at them from deep within the asylum's hallways. The walls themselves felt as if they were wailing in sorrow.

"What was that?" Timmy whispered into his microphone as he swung his camera toward the direction of the new sound. "It's like...It's like it's mourning."

Josh nodded solemnly, scanning the monitors for any sign that might explain what had just happened outside their experience or understanding.

"The audio sensors," he said at last. "It's real, not just our imaginations." He paused, then added: "Or it's making us hear what it wants us to hear."

While they were considering the option, a sudden movement caught their eyes. Before vanishing, it went past one of the thermal cameras with a distinct human-like shadow that is impossible to misidentify. The thing was purposeful in its motion and moved towards the deep parts of the asylum which had not yet been explored.

In a mixture of scientific curiosity and fear tinged caution Melinda said, "follow it" she continued "we may be led to something… some hint about what's going on here."

Josh acknowledged then picked up a hand held camera and started moving towards where he had seen the shadow take off accompanied by Timmy. Meanwhile Melinda stayed behind ensuring communication and monitoring equipment.

The corridors were twisty passages revealing more of the buildings haunted history at each turn; corroded bed frames, peeling paint, restraints leftovers and faded ominous stains on floors etcetera. Advancing made air cooler making their breaths visible in flashlight beams.

“Over here,” Timmy said pointing slightly opened door while Josh approached with his camera leveled at opening then pushed it open; there was rush of air as soon as he did so carrying antiseptic smell mixed faintly metallic-blood perhaps long dried but never forgettable.

The flashlight illuminated rows upon empty shelves with single overturned wheel chair in middle room felt charged as though past agonies echoed within its heaviness hung around them like specter energy they now found themselves amongst momentarily causing brief flicker from cameralight signifying such.

With every old record they find scattered about dark operations become clear- patients were more prisoners treated cruelly almost beyond recognition humane. Shadows seemed to lean closer breathing filled with whispers while investigator blurred into witness; each step forward through heart delving deeper into past that never gives up its secrets fully aware yet only beginning understanding jigsaw puzzle like nature these discoveries represent.

Indeed, Josh and Timmy were no strangers when it came to exploring abandoned medical rooms; however, this one felt different. There was a sense of stillness in the air that made it hard to breathe, let alone think straight. The shelving units lining each wall had once held bottles upon bottles of medicine, but now only dust and the occasional forgotten vial remained. The wheelchair, sitting smack dab in the middle of the floor with one wheel several feet away from its frame, seemed to symbolize everything wrong with this place.

This room was colder than any hallway they had passed through so far – colder even than the morgue. Josh's breath fogged up in his flashlight beam as he carefully stepped over debris. "It's like… it's been waiting for us," he murmured into his handheld camera.

Timmy nodded without looking up from his own camera work. "Yeah," he said simply – no elaboration needed.

Melinda was sitting at her temporary command post, watching the live feed from their cameras on her laptop. Her heart pounded in her chest as they traveled deeper into the bowels of the asylum. Checking the environmental readings, she noticed that the temperature had dropped significantly upon entering this room. "Be careful," she warned over her headset. "Something's not right about that room. It's way colder than anything we've seen so far."

Josh stopped to sift through a stack of old papers that littered the floor around a toppled filing cabinet. Wearing gloves, he lifted one carefully and tried to make out the faded text. "These are patient records," he said with a mix of fascination and horror in his voice. "It looks like treatment notes, but... these aren't treatments, they're... experiments."

Timmy zoomed in on the page where the words 'Hydrotherapy' and 'Electroshock' were both heavily underlined in shaky handwriting. "This is more than proof of hauntings," Timmy said soberly. "It's an abuse history, maybe even what's fueling them."

While they were documenting their findings, a sound filled the room — soft, sorrowful sobbing that seemed to come from nowhere and everywhere at once. Their cameras whipped toward its source as both men froze still. The sobbing grew louder, more anguished — it felt like the room was living its own tortured past.

"Melinda, are you getting this?" Josh whispered into his microphone without taking his eyes off where he thought the sound was coming from.

"Yes," Melinda answered breathlessly as audio meters on her screen spiked with each sob. "Yes it's recording all of this."

The crying eventually slowed down before stopping altogether — leaving behind silence that was heavy with unspoken words and stifled cries; silence that made every inch of that small room feel smaller, as if it contracted with the end of the sobbing and pressed down on them.

Josh packed up the papers, sliding them carefully into a bag. “We need to take these back, analyze them,” he said. “There might be names, dates… something that can help us figure out who these spirits are, what happened to them.”

Just as they were about to exit the room, an intense chill swept through — so cold that frost appeared to form on metal surfaces around them. The beams of their flashlights flickered for a moment before stabilizing; but when they did, the shadows seemed to linger longer than before, cling closer.

On their way back to Melinda now, their minds racing with everything they had just witnessed. The asylum — a house of pain and despair — was not just haunted but haunted by very real specters; every step back toward center weighted heavier with sorrow and grew more anxious about continuing presence there might provoke.

Chapter 12:
Night of Horrors

The atmosphere in Whitmore Asylum became thicker and thicker as the clock neared twelve midnight, every wall seemed to close around them. The silence was full of creaks and groans from everywhere in the old building, shadows becoming more intense as night went deeper.

The group gathered back at the main hall, considering it a central point where they could base their investigation on. Here was set up the Phantom Cage, which flickered inconsistently like its light was fighting against something invisible. Melinda watched the readings; they were showing spikes that had not been there before.

"We shouldn't have come here," she whispered without looking away from the screens. "It's different — this place is different; it knows we're here."

Josh kept checking their equipment setups over and over again, trying to appear calm even though his hands trembled with cold that had seeped into his bones. "We can handle this," he said, but he did not sound convince himself.

Timmy was fidgety; after every few seconds of capturing shots with his camera he would stare out into one dark corridor or another that branched off from the main hall. "There's something moving out there," he said almost too quietly to be heard, pointing his flashlight shakily toward an open doorway leading into blackness.

A gust of wind blew through the hall just then, a low wail riding on its back that made them all freeze — because it sounded human; because it sounded sad. It was followed by shadows swarming across walls so thickly that they didn't block light but rather swallowed it whole, leaving patches of darker darkness that moved and reached.

Equipment started malfunctioning: screens going haywire; Phantom Cage emitting a high-pitched keening sound that set their teeth on edge. Melinda scrambled to adjust settings but knew something else was happening now, beyond her understanding.

"It's reacting to us," Josh said out loud, "or we're triggering it."

They never had a chance to finish their conversation. Each member of the trio was suddenly overwhelmed by a physical representation of their worst fear. Water began rising in the room around Josh — just like on that day when he almost drowned as a child. He gasped for breaths, thrashed against something that wasn't there.

The walls started closing in on Melinda; she'd always been afraid of being alone. The room shrank, ceilings lowered, space turned into a tight box which pressed her from every side. She took shallow breaths, tried not to let claustrophobia claw over sanity.

For Timmy — who had always dreaded being abandoned — shadows became his loved ones one after another; each walked away from him into darkness with turned back till he was left behind calling them names that got swallowed by ever-encroaching dark.

In his panic and disorientation, Timmy stumbled away from the main hall dropping his camera in his haste to escape the sights of abandonment. His footsteps echoed hollowly as he vanished into the dark corridors of the asylum.

Understanding that something was wrong but not knowing what, Josh and Melinda each snapped out of their own terrifying experiences at about the same time and realized that Timmy was gone. "Timmy!" Josh called out, grabbing a flashlight and heading in the direction he had last seen him go.

Melinda composed herself quickly, but stayed close to Josh out of fear of being left alone. They moved through the dark calling for Timmy but there was no answer; only their voices echoed back at them from the empty halls which whispered silently around them.

Their flashlights barely pierced the blackness of the asylum as they searched desperately for Timmy. Each room they checked was empty, and with every passing moment dread gnawed at them more deeply as they continued on deeper into this night of terrors.

Josh and Melinda's frantic calls for Timmy bounced off crumbling walls in Whitmore Asylum's labyrinthine corridors, growing more desperate with each shout. Their flashlights danced shadows eerily across peeling paint and through barred windows that seemed to mock their efforts. The air turned colder than before, thickened by an oppressive mist that clung to their clothes like ectoplasmic residue and chilled their skin.

The building seemed to react to their presence as they pressed forward. Doors slammed shut with sudden force where before they had been standing wide open, and somewhere far away came a splintering crash as if glass had shattered against cold stone walls. Each new noise intensified their anxiety, making it seem like some malevolent presence lurked within these walls – a presence aware of them now more than ever under cover of night.

"This place… it's like a maze designed to confuse and trap," gasped Melinda, her scientific mind having trouble coping with the terror that pulsed through her.

Josh, equally scared but not about to give up on finding Timmy, tried to mark their path by making small scratches into the wooden door frames with his pocketknife. "We're not going to get lost," he told Melinda even though he himself was starting to doubt this.

Their search led them down another identical hallway and into the old hydrotherapy rooms – a notorious spot within the asylum where many of its cruelest treatments had been carried out. The door creaked ominously as they pushed it open, revealing a room lined with rusted tubs and broken tiles. Water dripped from a series of shattered pipes in a steady rhythm that joined other unsettling sounds echoing around them.

"Timmy?" Josh's voice cracked as he shone his flashlight onto a tub that was filled with murky water for some reason; but which reflected no light back at him from its still surface. As he approached it, a figure rose up from within — water cascading over what seemed to be human features, only horribly distorted and wrong

Melinda grabbed hold of Josh's arm and yanked him toward her just as the figure reached out for them, its touch like a vacuum sucking warmth from the air. "Not real!" she breathed, her words frosting in the cold. "It's trying to fool us, scare us off!"

They backed out of the room. The figure sank back into the water slowly, until it appeared to have never been there at all, except for the chill in their bones.

Shaken but undeterred, they pressed on, hardening themselves against the horrors of the asylum. As they turned a corner, Melinda's flashlight flickered and died; Josh's light cast a narrow beam down a stretch of hallway lined with old patient rooms. Soft murmurs could be heard behind closed doors — whispers of past agonies that still inhabited this place.

Suddenly, a loud crash echoed from the end of the hallway; a door swung violently open. Timmy lurched out from within the darkened room — pale-faced and wide-eyed with terror. "Josh! Melinda!" he cried out as he rushed toward them.

They closed ranks around him quickly, holding him tight. Timmy trembled against them; his camera was gone; his clothes were damp; his breath came raggedly. "I saw it — I saw what haunts us," he gasped between sobs, his earlier courage evaporated into the asylum air.

While they comforted him, it occurred to all three that leaving wasn't just an option anymore — it was a matter of self-preservation. They had to get out not only with their findings intact but with their sanity and lives as well.

In silence and haste they made their way back through pitch-black corridors to where they'd first entered Whitmore Asylum's main hall. But — unknown to them — there is one more secret this place has yet to reveal: one last terror that awaits them as they try to untangle the nightmarish reality which has enveloped them, and pushes their psychological and physical limits to the breaking point.

Josh moved ahead with his only flashlight still working, attempting to retrace their steps back to the main hall from where they were through the use of markers. But something was wrong with the layout; everything seemed a little bit off, familiar things a little bit different. "This doesn't make any sense," he ground out in frustration as they came across a door, they had marked earlier that had been bricked over with old red bricks that were crumbling but solid.

The air was thick with an oppressive smell of mold and rot, making every breath feel like work. It was as if the history of screams from this place could be seen etched into the walls themselves, hovering on the coldness that wrapped around them. When they passed by treatment rooms one after another, the door to electroshock therapy swung open with a creak into nothing but blackness so deep it might have gone all the way down to hell itself. They hurried past without looking too closely.

Then there was a scream – piercing through corridors like knives, sharp and full of fear; it stopped them dead in their tracks. "Did you hear that?" Melinda's voice tightened with fear as she scanned down dimly lit corridor behind them. They held their breaths and listened but heard nothing more than silence – just on other side of hearing: faint whisper carried by cold wind that brushed past them like somebody talking but not quite being able to make out what is said.

They pressed on until at last saw exit light glowing faintly green far away down some final stretch – promise of freedom outside this nightmare world they stumbled into hours ago now coming within reach at last. But when they got closer, light started flickering like mad and ground beneath them shook. Dust and small debris rained from ceiling upon heads as low rumbling grew into deafening roar. Walls seemed alive, undulating inwardly outwardly as though breathing giant beast's chest.

"The building—it's reacting!" Melinda cried out, grabbing onto both Josh and Timmy as they sprinted toward exit.

But doors seemed to recede like somebody elongating hallway by magic . Lungs burned with exertion and fear – every gasp filled with dusty, stale air of asylum they have been breathing for past several hours.

Finally reaching them, Josh threw himself into doors with all his weight behind it, bursting through to cold early morning air outside. They spilled out onto front steps overgrown with weeds and ivy, where dawn chill bit at their sweat-soaked bodies and made them shiver. Behind them doors slammed closed hard enough to make whole building shake little – sound that struck trio as final in some way or another.

They collapsed on steps after what felt like eternity spent running for lives, panting like dogs who had just finished chasing rabbits through fields of tall grass until tongues lolled half out mouths. First light began creeping up over horizon casting long shadows across asylum's facade; now silent in its deathly stillness – might not ever have known about restful sleep since it was built. But this didn't matter anymore because those three knew better than anyone else alive that night could never be forgotten nor forgiven.

Chapter 13: Crack

The Whitmore Asylum grounds felt abnormally quiet under the dim glow of early morning. It was as if the world was holding its breath. The two of them had only stopped for a moment, exhausted in both body and spirit from what they'd seen and experienced during the night. But that pause, brief as it was, had been long enough for an unspoken agreement to pass between them: they couldn't just leave Timmy's disappearance unexplained, his fate unknown. So they went back in. And the stink of decay and fear came rushing out to greet them like an old friend.

They took their time getting down to the basement. Each step colder than the last; each footfall heavier with the weight of so many stories stacked on top of one another. Josh's flashlight flickered at Melinda from up ahead, fighting against whatever pushed back at it from within those walls – and losing more often than not. She clutched her own light, knuckles white around it; kept looking over her shoulder at all those shifting shapes just outside its beam.

Down here were all these old storage rooms and forgotten spaces filled with forgotten things – discarded medical equipment; files upon files upon boxes upon shelves – and somewhere off in the distance a sink dripped slow and steady like water torture for ghosts. All empty when checked; all abandoned long ago; all choked with dust so thick you could taste its neglect hanging heavy in the air.

And then there was this one part further removed from the rest of everything, even down here in this basement, where maybe they once stored something big or bad or both – because there were chains fastened deep into some walls here that hadn't been used for anything good in a very long time; because there were windows set high into others that had bars across them too thick to see through or break free from. It was here that they found what was left of Timmy.

He was slumped against the far wall, his camera shattered beside him. The scene was brutal; his injuries were many and varied, and no cause for any of them could be determined. It looked as if some incredible force had just ripped through the room, slashing its way to nowhere in particular. His clothes were torn, and there were dark stains on the concrete all around him.

Melinda gasped – clapped a hand over her mouth –and Josh fell to his knees beside Timmy while she backed away from it all, her flashlight's beam shaking so hard you'd think it was scared of the truth – which was that this one room with those few walls around them ain't where they are anymore. No: now they're trapped inside four walls within four other walls that keep getting closer no matter how far apart they may seem. And each one is painted with a different shade of bad memories that can't be scrubbed off or covered up or wished away.

Josh checked for a pulse anyway; held his hand to Timmy's shoulder anyway; hoped for a miracle anyway. "No, no, no" he muttered through clenched teeth when he found none.

The sight of it turned Melinda's stomach – sent her backing further into herself until she almost wasn't there at all anymore; until she almost couldn't see anything at all anymore except for tears – while around them this one little room in this one big house started to close its doors tighter than ever before; started to squeeze down harder than ever before on anyone left inside – because there's something about pain that tells stories better than words ever could; something about fear that makes everything feel alive even when it isn't anymore.

"We can't leave him like this," said Josh after a while, voice hollow. He looked up at Melinda then, eyes red-rimmed and haunted. "We have to bring him back. We have to tell his family."

She nodded, wiped her eyes with the back of her hand – palm still shaking so hard it made more tears spill over onto her cheeks. "Yeah," she whispered into the silence of that place that used to be a room but now was something else entirely; her phone clattered out of her pocket then, and she had to pick it up off the floor twice before she could get a grip on it – once because her hands were shaking too much, and once because everything was pitch black now.

They sat there in silence with Timmy, waiting for the emergency services to show up. Josh and Melinda didn't speak. What had happened was horrible. They couldn't have thought of a worse way for their friend's life to end. It felt like a wound to their very souls; it showed them how stupidly they'd toyed with danger.

The first responders come out of the basement into the harsh, unwelcoming early morning light. Every step away from the building, through the asylum's gates, feels like a step back towards reality — but a different reality than it was before. One that they wish they could forget. The ride back to campus is silent; each person is lost in their own thoughts — haunted by memories; shadowed by grief. There's no going back now; supernatural forces and human frailty widened the fracture in their lives into a chasm.

Josh and Melinda sat next to Timmy's lifeless body as sirens broke through the quiet of the early morning. Their minds were numb, each fighting against an onslaught of emotions that threatened to drown them both. There was no comfort on the cold floor of this basement; only pain made visible under unforgiving fluorescent lights carried by unfeeling hands.

A team of paramedics and police officers enters the basement with great urgency following closely behind them are more police cars with flashing lights and blaring sirens filling up any empty space arounds this old building Which seemed even older at this time of day due mostly because there hasn't been any sunlight getting inside for years except through broken windows which doesn't help much either what little does manage To penetrate these dark corridors can't possibly reach far enough into them now not so deep after all just barely scratching surface really officer who appears be charge quickly assesses situation then turns his attention towards Josh who had taken upon himself keep vigil over his fallen friend

“We need to secure this area” he says with a firmness of someone who knows what has done this before as if it’s not enough that they found themselves in an abandoned asylum basement filled with dead bodies but now there could also be otherworldly forces still at work here which is why he wants no stone left unturned so while one officer begins taping off the crime scene another takes out his phone and starts recording everything on video detective approaches Melinda asking her questions about what happened tonight.

The journey back to the university was a silent one, with each person lost in their own thoughts. Outside her window, Melinda stared vacantly at a blur of colors that never quite resolved into anything. Beside her, Josh kept his eyes fixed on the road ahead, his jaw set tight and a storm of anger brewing under his calm exterior. The unfairness of Timmy’s death, the questions about what had really happened — what they had done — burned inside him like acid.

The sun was fully up by the time they got back to campus, its light harsh and unforgiving. They split at the medical center without needing to say anything; there were no words left for this shared trauma that bound them together but also kept them painfully apart. Melinda dragged herself back to her dorm slowly, mechanically putting one foot in front of the other as if she could outrun or outwalk the night's horrors.

Josh couldn't bring himself to go home yet, so he found himself wandering aimlessly around campus in the early morning stillness. The library where he'd spent so many nights studying for exams seemed foreign now, as did every other building he passed by. He was seeing it all through some kind of twisted funhouse mirror.

As Josh and Melinda struggle to process what happened during those endless hours at Whitmore Asylum — when they were looking for proof and found something far darker than either of them bargained for — life churns on around them. Oblivious or indifferent to everything that swallowed Timmy and threatened to swallow them too, people are beginning their day with no idea how close they came last night to being devoured alive.

With students and faculty starting to move around more freely now that daylight has arrived and banished most evils back into their hiding places, Josh finds himself sitting on a secluded bench near the botanical gardens. He and Timmy used to come here sometimes after marathon research sessions to clear their heads. Now every leaf and flower seems to taunt Josh with its peace.

The sky is bright and clear, but it might as well be overcast for all the light that's getting through Josh's shock and mourning. The sounds of laughter and snatches of far-off conversation, usually so comforting from his bench by the student center, are distant and alien now. They reach him muffled, like he's on the other side of a thick glass wall.

Back in her room at last, Melinda finds no comfort in the familiar confines of her private space. If anything, it feels smaller than ever tonight. Her workstation — covered in notes, data charts, scrawled-out ideas from their investigations — is a monument to failure. With shaking hands, she starts gathering up papers and methodically feeding them into her shredder: dedication turning to desperation turning to need.

Her phone rings — classmates, professors who've heard rumors of an incident — but she can't bring herself to answer any of them. Words would be meaningless right now anyway. She just draws her curtains closed against a world that won't stop shining its cruel light into her eyes and crawls into bed with the covers pulled over her head.

Josh's phone buzzed in his pocket. He paid no attention to it, scrolling through the last few texts from Timmy instead -- a boring conversation about supplies needed for the investigation. Every word was like a punch in the gut: Timmy was dead, and they were at fault. They had gone too far, too fast; intoxicated by discovery, they believed they could control what lay beyond their understanding.

By mid-morning, shock had given way to a sickening dread. What would they tell Timmy's family? How could they possibly explain any of this? And past the mourning and self-loathing loomed the threat of what they'd stirred up. Was it done with them or had they opened a door that couldn't be closed?

Hours later, when campus security found Josh still sitting stiffly on the bench by Building C — his face ashen, eyes blank — they approached with caution. "Mr. Carter," one officer began gently after consulting her clipboard. "We need you to come with us." She offered him a hand up from the cold metal seat. "There are some formalities we have to take care of … and we think maybe you could use some help too."

Wordlessly Josh nodded and rose shakily to his feet; he felt like his legs might give out beneath him at any moment.

As Josh is led into the campus health center, memories and regrets whirl through his mind's eye like debris in a storm drain; while alone in her dim bedroom Melinda wrestles with her own demons of logic over irrational nightmares made real; but it is through them both that one feels most keenly this sense of having been wrapped in layers upon layer of suffocating cotton wool which leach all color out from everything leaving only each passing second an echo forever reminding them of that darkness which has come before — even now fearing what may still lie there waiting unseen just beyond sight — the horror of the asylum not so easily escaped from.

Chapter 14:
Spiraling Downwards

After the tragedy at Whitmore Asylum, Josh and Melinda's lives fell apart. Grief and guilt unraveled every thread of familiarity and academic ambition they had. Around them, the campus buzzed on, ignorant of the deep damage that had been dealt to two students who walked its paths like phantoms among the living.

Their third friend, Josh — once a paragon of resolve and leadership among them — began to retreat into himself. His apartment became a cave, curtains perpetually drawn, dim light staining everything he owned; hours upon hours were spent in silence sitting still replaying everything in his head. The last few panicked shouts from Timmy echoing off the walls; his own voice insisting they would find him; all haunting him without rest. Sleep came in sporadic bursts of nightmare that left him waking up alone in the dark gasping for air with cold sweat sticking to his skin.

When it was light out, Josh hardly went to class anymore; when he did there was noticeable dissonance between him and everyone else. He sat as far back as possible but even then couldn't hear what the professor said over the roar of whatever godforsaken thing was dwelling just beneath where consciousness meets subconsciousness in his mind. Talking to classmates devolved into a kind of game kids play when one only knows monosyllabic words: "Yeah." "No." "Okay." Not only did this fail to get across whatever message Josh was supposed to want people around him understanding but it also pushed away whatever empathy or sympathy had initially begun emanating from those same people — after a while their tentative attempts at closeness died off entirely because no matter how you approach someone who is so clearly suffering there is always some wall between you if they won't talk back.

Melinda's symptoms were different from Josh's but no less severe. Her world used to be so neat, but now her dorm room was a mess of scattered papers and unwashed clothes. The once-rigid scientist who thrived on control found herself unable to decide or do anything at all; deadlines for research papers and class assignments came and went while Melinda stared blankly at words she couldn't process on her computer screen.

Food became an afterthought — either forgotten entirely or skipped over with a cup of coffee in the morning that would only last until nighttime when she would realize she hadn't eaten all day. Her body deteriorated along with her mind: cheeks hollowed out, eyes sunk deep into her skull, skin pale enough to see through under the right light.

Friends and roommates tried to help but grew ever more helpless as Melinda's behavior became increasingly erratic. She jumped at every little sound — closing doors and footsteps in the hall sent her into fights-or-flight panic mode; talking about Timmy or making any reference at all to their project caused an instant emotional shutdown or worse, sometimes, violent outbursts that left her shaking in tears.

One night a friend found Melinda sitting alone in the dark muttering words like "spectral" and "containment failures" to herself. They realized then just how far gone she really was and called university counseling services demanding immediate attention be given to their friend's case.

In therapy sessions there were just fragments of sentences about the asylum here or there; bits and pieces about Timmy mixed in with descriptions of shadows which kept drifting around corners of vision — blending memories up against present reality until it became nearly impossible telling one apart from other anymore; hints dropped intermittently throughout talks regarding suicide attempts past yet future planned for nights soon approaching; everything garbled so much that even seasoned professionals had trouble making sense most days but occasionally spoke phrases like "severe PTSD" and "intensive therapy"

Josh knew about Melinda's situation and was filled with guilt once again. He had shut himself off from the world while she suffered by herself. Under the weight of his own depression, he agreed to go with her to therapy, hoping it would be a step toward recovering from—or at least making sense of—their shared trauma.

So here they are, sitting together yet light years apart in their first joint therapy session. The room is quiet except for the soft ticking of the clock on the wall and intermittent laughter from students outside—a reminder of what used to be. As they begin to untangle their story, it becomes painfully clear how far they've fallen, and how much further they have to climb.

In Dr. Emerson's office, Josh and Melinda might as well be on another planet. It is dark outside; the walls are beige and bare save for a few framed certificates; the furniture is functional but impersonal. Dr. Emerson listens intently as they tell their stories in pieces: one person starts a phrase, trails off into nothingness, then stares out into space while the other picks up where they left off.

Josh sits rigidly upright in his chair, hands balled so tightly between his knees that his knuckles have turned white. His voice is flat as he describes what happened—just the facts—like he's reading someone else's case file. It's self-preservation: if he keeps it clinical, maybe it won't hurt so bad.

Melinda can't seem to sit still at all; she alternates between silence so deep you can hear it humming against your eardrums and words that come pouring out like an overturned dam—an avalanche of fear and confusion and guilt. Her hands twist a tissue into an ever-tightening spiral; her eyes dart frantically around the room, searching every shadow for monsters that only she can see.

Dr. Emerson knows how to pace them; she's done this dance many times before. "What were you feeling right then?" she asks gently when they find themselves back in the hallway after Timmy disappeared, or "Do you think the shadows have followed you here?" when Melinda mentions that word.

For a moment, these questions tether them to the ground where they sit, their backs hunched against an unseen precipice. But a question is a dangerous thing—it peels away layers of protection until all that's left is raw nerve and wounded flesh.

Finally, near the end of the session, Josh breaks. His voice cracks as he speaks: "I should have stopped us. I should have seen it coming. It's my fault Timmy's gone." Tears spill over onto his cheeks—tears he didn't know were there until he said those words aloud.

Melinda reaches out—an arm's length or two but it might as well be a bridge across an ocean—and her hand shakes as she touches Josh's arm. It is the smallest gesture in the world, but it speaks volumes about what they've been through together and how deeply it has scarred them both. "We all missed them," she says quietly. "We pushed too hard."

Dr. Emerson nods; she has seen this shift happen a thousand times before. "It's important to remember that responsibility is shared," she says gently, "and that guilt isn't always a reliable measure of truth when we're dealing with trauma."

Naming the following sessions for continued therapy, doctor Emerson highlighted both individual and joint healing. According to her, personal traumas as well as new dynamics caused by the incident should be addressed too. In addition, she prescribed mild sedatives which will help them manage anxiety and sleep better given that rest is vital during recovery.

Upon their emergence from the therapist's office into the campus of a typical day – students rushing between classes, laughing with friends – Josh and Melinda sat heavily on a bench. They walked in silence until they found a spot where they could sit and think.

Sitting there in the early afternoon sun, long shadows stretching across the quad before them; sitting there while their words moved slowly away from what was revealed at their morning appointment toward how they might get through another day: it became clear that neither of them could think any further ahead than attending class more often or meeting for coffee once a week to talk about everything other than ghosts and monsters; but even so, this knowledge carried no weight against all they had seen and felt.

So they sat there quietly while leaves rustled around their feet, and autumn breezes tugged at jackets that were never warm enough – watching as students tossed frisbees across open fields, caught up in laughter that seemed to float along on invisible currents: ordinary scenes from another lifetime.

Melinda shivered beside him. It wasn't cold—not really—but she pulled her jacket tighter anyway. Out of habit more than anything else. And then she looked at him – really looked at him – and saw how exhausted he was; how much older his face seemed since three months ago when they first met. "Do you think we'll ever be normal again?" she asked softly.

Josh turned his head toward her voice, hope flickering behind his eyes like a candle flame struggling against its glass prison walls. He blinked his answer into existence: "I don't know...but I think we have to try. For Timmy's sake – and ours – we've got to find some way back."

They stayed like that for a while, side by side but lost in their own thoughts. Josh understood that the therapist had meant small steps, not giant leaps. “Maybe...maybe we could start by going back to the lab?” he suggested, each word gathering strength as it left his mouth. “Not to work—not yet—but just...to clean up. To pack everything away. To close that book, literally and figuratively.”

Melinda nodded slowly. She understood what he was saying; she’d felt it as well. “Yeah,” she agreed at last, her voice barely louder than the breeze rustling through nearby trees (a sound almost…peaceful). “Maybe...maybe seeing it as just...as just a room again will make it easier to move past this.”

Deciding that enough time had been spent sitting and thinking, they stood up from the bench with effort and began making their way back toward the science building - slower this time; more deliberate. They avoided the shortcut past the library with its connotations of ghosts and demons lurking within its walls, opting instead for a longer route: one which would give them more time to steel themselves before walking through that door again-

As they moved in, the smell of antiseptic and old books hit them — a scent that had always been comforting. This was what their first days at university used to smell like: curiosity and academic drive. Back before everything changed. Josh stopped at the lab door, hand on the knob, took a deep breath, and pushed.

Inside, it looked just as they had left it: papers everywhere, equipment still set up, spectral phenomena notes scribbled across a whiteboard. But in the daytime and with new eyes, it didn't look so much like a center for scientific inquiry as it did after the storm has passed.

They went about cleaning methodically. Melinda sorted through the papers, deciding which ones needed to be kept and which could be shredded. Josh took apart the Phantom Cage piece by piece; every fragment was another piece of their overambitious failure. They worked mostly in silence because there wasn't much to say — each movement was one step closer to untangling all those memories from each object.

And slowly but surely things started looking more like they used to — a place of learning and discovery rather than fear and loss. It happened gradually, painfully at times as when Timmy's camera came into view again, broken beyond repair this time around and buried beneath layers of dust.

When they're done cleaning up the lab there is a slight lift in their spirits — something about clearing out the physical space feels like progress or healing or whatever you want to call it. Locking up behind them on their way out is purely symbolic for having survived that haunted chamber; leaving an open grave behind you should never feel so satisfying. But then again they've only taken a few steps down the hallway when there's no denying that both footsteps are echoing off empty walls now instead of just one side like before — closing chapters is supposed to echo throughout entire buildings not just single rooms filled with ghosts who won't let go.

While one chapter has closed, they understand that the journey of recovery is filled with unseen challenges and memories.

Chapter 15: Prophecy

With the lab behind them and the setting sun at their back, Josh and Melinda made their way across campus towards the administration building. The weight of the last few days hung on them, slowing their steps. Professor Eldridge had called for them after hearing what they'd been through, and now they were going to see him.

"I can't believe we might have opened a — "Melinda began.

"Portal?" Josh finished. "It sounds like a bad sci-fi movie. But after everything…" He shook his head. They had been too close to it all to keep denying that something impossible had happened.

Melinda nodded slowly as if trying to understand it all herself. "Every time we used the app, the activity increased," she said aloud, her voice filled with both scientific curiosity and fear. "We thought we were just detecting the phenomena, not…not facilitating it."

Josh's brow furrowed in thought. "And those spikes in the data every time we turned it on…it wasn't just detection," he realized out loud, feeling like a bucket of cold water was being poured over his head. "It was interaction."

When they reached Professor Eldridge's office — an imposing room filled with books and artifacts from his long career in science and studying paranormal occurrences — he looked up at them from behind his large oak desk with sharp eyes that seemed to demand respect from everyone around him.

"Joshua," he greeted nodding once before turning his gaze towards Melinda and giving her a small smile so full of warmth that she felt herself blush under its weight.

"You've been through quite a bit I hear," he said starting off with more than a touch of sadness lacing into each word spoken as if they held secrets known only between friends who had seen far too many battles together already.

The room smelled thickly of old leather and paper; none of those college books had ever left his side for very long. Gesturing towards the chairs in front of his desk, Eldridge sighed heavily before continuing.

"What you've stumbled upon, what you've…" He paused here searching for the right words to describe it all and landed on none before finally settling on a simple truth that he could be certain about sharing with others who had come so far down this road already. "We were part of a project during the early days of spectral research. Our findings were promising — they still are, even now — but we quickly realized the dangers."

Melinda's eyes perked up at this, her exhaustion temporarily forgotten as she leaned forward in her seat. "So you knew about the portal effects?"

The professor's face darkened with regret as he nodded slowly. "Yes," he said simply, avoiding her gaze entirely because sometimes there were no answers to give except for ones that would only lead to more questions being asked in return.

"Then why wasn't it documented? Why didn't we know?" Josh demanded bitterly.

Eldridge sighed again and rubbed his temples tiredly; there was so much explaining left to do and not nearly enough energy within him anymore to see it through properly without giving into exhaustion completely.

"The records were sealed — classified even within our own circles," he explained quietly while looking straight ahead at nothing particular sitting just beyond those walls which held secrets better left undisturbed by curious minds like theirs. "We feared knowledge falling into wrong hands or worse someone else trying what we did." His voice dropped low here because some things were best spoken about only when absolutely necessary – like speaking ill of dead men who may or may not haunt one's nightmares forever afterwards. "And after what we saw…" The sentence trailed off into silence as though words would do no justice in describing everything that had happened when they thought all hope had been lost forevermore.

Josh shivered at this, his shoulders hunching forward as if trying to ward off some unseen chill that now clung to him like a second skin. “You should have warned us.”

Eldridge met Josh’s gaze with his own, the weight of all he’d seen in this life etched deep into those wrinkles which lined either side of his face from years spent studying things best left alone by men who valued their sanity above all else.

“I thought enough time had passed,” the old man said finally, voice raw but steady. “I thought maybe with new technology…better safeguards…”

“But you were wrong,” Josh spat bitterly.

The professor nodded slowly; there was no point in arguing with someone whose wounds were still fresh even if they hadn’t been physically inflicted upon them directly by Eldridge himself.

“Yes,” he admitted quietly while looking down at his hands which were now folded neatly atop one another on top of that large oak desk before him. “Yes, I was wrong.”

Josh frowned deeply at this because sometimes apologies just weren’t enough anymore — not when someone else had paid for those mistakes with their very life.

Their shared weighty confessions hung in the room and paused the conversation. The sun began to set, stretching the shadows further outside and casting an orange light through the window.

“What now?” Melinda asked, her mind whirling with implications. “If we really did open a gateway, how do we close it?”

“I’ve been thinking about that since you started your experiments,” Professor Eldridge said. “I think with proper preparation and understanding, we can find a way to close it together. But it’s going to be dangerous, and I wouldn’t blame you for walking away after everything you’ve been through.”

Josh looked at Melinda and they had a silent conversation. After a moment he said, “We have to fix this. Not just for Timmy – so that it never happens to anyone again.”

They start planning, drawing on all of the professor’s previous research and their recent experiences; outside night falls and the campus grows still as most students retreat into their dorms, leaving them alone in the professor’s office for what may be their greatest – or last – experiment.

As twilight slid into evening, Professor Eldridge's office seemed to shrink in upon itself. The light retreated against advancing corners of shadow that crept in from unseen places as if hungry. Josh couldn't say where those creeping shades went; if asked he would have said ‘away’ but not known what he meant by that answer either - only felt right about saying so much without knowing why except how much it mattered not knowing but wanting more than anything else now here then there beyond etcetera or suchlike words which were themselves too quiet during these hours when you could almost hear silence speak louder than whispers ever might do next time around maybe perhaps who knows who cares oh well fine whatever okay right yes sure no problem maybe later tomorrow yesterday forevermore Amen Hallelujah Holy Cow Etcetera.

The atmosphere was electrified. The professor spread out his old research notes and diagrams, which had been kept under lock and key for decades, on a desk cluttered with ancient books and faded papers that seemed to whisper secrets of their own.

He pointed a shaky hand at a particularly worn map; its edges were frayed and the lines were faded. "This," he said, "is the theoretical overlay of the spectral and physical realms. We identified points of convergence based on geomagnetic forces and historical sightings of paranormal activity." His finger tapped on several locations that formed an almost perfect circle around what would have been the Whitmore Asylum. "It’s not coincidental that you picked that place; it's a natural weak point between worlds—a focal point."

Melinda leaned over the map, her eyes following along the lines, absorbing what this meant. "So these convergence points are like natural doorways? And our app didn’t just detect—it boosted up an existing breach?"

"Yes," nodded Eldridge gravely. "Your device acted as a catalyst by accident - it made bigger both reach & power of opened portal."

Josh rubbed his temples; they had too much responsibility now. "How do we undo it? Can't we at least weaken or close off this gateway?"

The professor produced another set of documents—these ones newer, filled with equations and complex diagrams. "Based on what I've seen before, plus everything you two have gone through… We might be able to create counter-frequency," he said. "Basically broadcasting anti-signals should stabilize or stop these portals from opening."

Melinda caught on to the scientific basis quickly. "We could modify Phantom Cage so it emits this frequency," she said slowly nodding her head. "But we'd need to do precise calculations & controls – it's risky."

They worked late into the night, drawing models and running simulations on Melinda's laptop. Now and then one of them would stop, lost in thought or overwhelmed by the magnitude of what they were doing. The room was quiet save for the barely audible scratching of pens on paper and the occasional murmur of conversation.

As they continued their work, it grew colder in the room — a reminder of the forces they were dealing with. Josh glanced at the window every so often, half-expecting to see something unspeakable looking back at him, but the night outside remained still and dark, save for the swaying branches of trees.

Hours later, after much arguing and planning, they had a plan for a prototype. They were tired; their eyes were blurry and movements slow as if underwater. But there was also a sense of triumph — perhaps even hope — that they could fix what they'd broken.

"We're going to have to test it at these points," Eldridge said finally, marking red Xs on convergence points across the map. "It's dangerous. You'll be stepping into an unknown."

"We know," said Josh. His voice was flat and deadened by exhaustion. "We're ready."

During that time, Melinda made her way back to the dorm room. She moved quickly and precisely while gathering her own equipment. For example, she checked her laptop again and made sure all of the software updates were configured to handle the data they might be collecting. She also packed personal protective equipment (PPE), such as salt, which was recommended in some of their readings as a basic deterrent against malevolent spirits. Although she wasn't entirely sold on its effectiveness, she wasn't going to take any chances either.

Meanwhile, Professor Eldridge returned to his office where he pulled out old files and texts from hidden compartments and locked drawers - materials that had not seen daylight in years but would undoubtedly prove crucial for their success. His hands shook slightly as he handled the faded papers; each one was a relic of a haunted past filled with perilous expeditions and earth-shattering revelations. Alongside these historical relics went his own set of tools and sensors; specialized equipment that hadn't been used since his last brush with the supernatural.

By mid-morning the team had regrouped at the lab, though the air was thick with anticipation (and anxiety). They spread out old maps and notes across several tables – makeshift command center style – marking each convergence point and discussing strategies for quickest/safest routes of access.

Their preparations were meticulous; Josh took charge of physically setting up the Phantom Cage itself (integrating new modifications that would hopefully enable them to emit counter-frequencies effectively) while Melinda worked alongside him calibrating software to control emissions & collect data simultaneously.

Throughout it all they discussed potential outcomes in technical jargon mixed with cautious optimism – failures acknowledged but quickly dismissed; no room for doubt at this stage in their mindset.

As the sun climbed higher in the sky casting its deceitful veneer over campus life below, so did tensions rise within confines of our make-shift laboratory headquarters here atop this hill overlooking it all. Final checks and preparations were made; each member of the team fully aware of history about to be confronted – dangers likely to be faced – and very real chance that their actions could alter forevermore boundary between known & unknown worlds.

As they loaded everything into the rented van for transport, a sense of finality hung heavy in the air; whatever comes next, their lives will never be the same. They drove off leaving behind familiar sights sounds & smells associated with university life; headed toward convergence points - toward confrontation with unknowable.

Chapter 16:
Extreme Steps

Under a cloudy, gray sky spanned an isolated university's remote storage facility, a bleak outline against the desolate land. Here among rows of discarded machines and forgotten experiments, Josh, Melinda and Professor Eldridge were about to take their most desperate action yet; they will destroy the app and all related technology completely.

The building is long and low with thick concrete walls and steel doors that were originally designed for hazardous scientific materials storage. But now it serves as the final resting place for the equipment that accidentally opened a gateway into another world.

When they stepped inside the cold echoing space, Melinda carried with her a metal box containing hard drives, USB sticks and her laptop – every piece of data and software connected to the app loaded into them. Her hands did not shake but her eyes told of great tiredness. Josh wheeled in a cartful of Phantom Cage parts which each represented some stage between fascination and terror.

Professor Eldridge led them through to what seemed like an incinerator room – places like this have been built to burn even indestructible materials down forever where they can't harm anyone anymore – "Everything must go" he said simply "Every line of code every circuit that made this app work"

Beyond its thick door lay darkness which smelled strongly burnt-metal-and-plastic-ly. Work began with a sense both urgent enough to be quick but final enough never needing repeating.

Josh took care not only physically destroying hardware; he unscrewed panels breaking circuits crushing chips one at time until none could ever function again then reduced Phantom Cage component by component from sophisticated device into scrap heap made up mostly wires surrounded by bits metal

Melinda paused before formatting hard drives wiping them clean with hammering sound she found hanging nearby but instead smashing each repeatedly until flat then dropping laptop on furnace deck whose glow had watched over much knowledge gained so far only ever leaving her side when necessary sacrifice had been called for

Professor Eldridge watched as smaller pieces USB sticks backup drives other storage devices were carefully placed into metal container which was then slid inside furnace "This is the only way" he said softly closing heavy door behind him before turning temperature up high

It did not take long for flames to leap alive licking everything around it devouring all that had been their focus these months; fire raged until nothing left but ashes so they stood side by side watching in silence knowing without speaking what else needs doing now but keep moving forward always forward never back down from whatever comes next because if not them then who?

They froze, rotating towards the noise. A dim light pushed its way out of the shadows at the far end of the hall, throbbing softly at first and then steadily brightening. It didn't look like a bulb — not warm and yellow — but rather cold and otherworldly, as though it came from everywhere and nowhere all at once.

"The portal," Josh said in a whisper, his voice full of disbelief. "It's not just on the app... it's here."

That it could exist outside their technology and become more entwined with reality dawns on them with horrifying clarity. With few choices remaining and time running short, they are forced to consider an even more extreme solution — one whose aftermath would stretch far beyond anything they had conceived.

Josh, Melinda, and Professor Eldridge stood rooted to the floor as the unnatural light grew brighter, casting strange shapes against the cold concrete of the storage facility. The air around them seemed heavier than before; there was a pressure that made breathing difficult. It was like watching a flame through water — sometimes flickering violently enough to distort its own shadow.

“What do we do now?” Melinda broke through the silence thick with dread; her fear was still present but tinged with defiance. They’d hoped destroying their technological pieces would break whatever connected this place to that one... but hope faded with each moment that persistent glow refused to wane.

The professor adjusted his glasses — older lines on his face deeper than ever before; eyes locked onto pulsating brightness — trying to steady himself for what he knew must come next. “We need understand this has latched itself onto local space-time independent our equipment; while our actions may have reduced its grip we appear not close off completely.”

Josh squeezed his fists together so hard veins popped out frustration mixed with terror filling up every square inch him until there wasn’t any room left for anything else except words of finality. “So we’re back at square one?” he asked, voice sharp as the edge of broken glass.

The professor sighed, shook his head a little bit — no; not entirely. “It’s open,” he said slowly, carefully picking apart each syllable like bad tooth far too late pull out. “But we didn’t know it could still stay open after what we’ve done... We now have critical information about our portal.”

“We know it’s not just our technology!” Melinda always scientist tried be pragmatic even when staring into face insanity itself — so she pulled out notebook started sketching layout facility surrounding area looked for telltale signs either possess geomagnetic properties or contain history relevant haunted houses and other spooky stories she’d read growing up.

As they spoke, the light began to change shape: stretching upwards until there was nothing left but a vertical slit cut through air in front of them like reality cracking under pressure, fabric normal world giving way unknown dimensions.

“This is getting worse.” Josh took step back involuntarily; his voice made clear that thing seemed grow him with each passing second.

The professor nodded grimly. “We may need consider some more... drastic measures. There are theories in field spectral phenomena which posit that breaches can be sealed but these require large amounts energy and carry their own set risks.”

“Such as?” Melinda didn’t look away from slit now expanding wider than doorway frame directly across aisle from where stood

"Risks that could involve changing the site's core characteristics—its magnetic and even dimensional properties. It is extremely experimental and may have wider effects on the surrounding environment,” Eldridge said gravely.

The decision pressed down on them. The danger of making such a huge move was terrifying, but so was the alternative—leaving a gateway open, possibly allowing more hostile beings into their world.

They were standing there talking about what they could do when suddenly the light from the portal started flashing in and out like a giant invisible creature's heart beating. It shone with an unearthly glow that drew them closer while pushing them away all at once.

Setting up a temporary research station right there in the storage facility had been Josh's idea. They brought all the remaining scientific instruments and materials they could find and began analyzing every aspect of the portal's properties. This became their new base—a makeshift lab where they might make a breakthrough or bring about their own destruction.

Josh, Melinda, and Professor Eldridge worked through the night, hunched over instruments whose readings were occasionally interrupted by flashes from the portal. The task was massive but fueled by mission-driven urgency: Every test brought them one step closer to solving this or realizing how wrong they were about everything.

In dim quarters of transformed storage space turned ad hoc lab for desperate science around an imminent event horizon stood Josh, Melinda, and Professor Eldridge under eye of otherworldly light emanating from pulsing gateway keeping watchful silence above; its depths seemingly alive with spider-like tendrils creeping along walls casting long boney shapes across uneven floorboards shadow-dancing beneath flickering industrial bulbs hanging loose by wires just overhead.

Around them equipment hummed and beeped as data on electromagnetic fields, spatial anomalies, and other environmental factors that might be affecting stability were collected. Whenever something changed Melinda jotted it down dutifully onto her laptop (her face illuminated by its screen's glow) where she cross-referenced current readings against theoretical models they had only ever discussed in the abstract.

Professor Eldridge leafed through ancient texts and modern papers alike, scattered across a folding table; searching for precedent or forgotten theory which might shed light on their plight. Every now and then he would mutter something—formula or historical reference—that sent Melinda scurrying to recalibrate instruments or revise procedure.

Josh busied himself with adjusting the physical setup around the portal; using what remained of Phantom Cage along with other salvaged tech he erected containment fields. His hands moved swiftly but with care born from knowing that each tweak brought them closer to sealing reality's wound or hastening its spread into nothingness.

The room was electric with tension, heavy ozone scent underscoring the fear of failure mingling with each breath drawn. The portal seemed to respond to their efforts, light ebbing and flowing like some vast creature's respiration

Once upon a time, while modifying a scanner by the edge of the opening, Josh inadvertently thrust his hand into the shining. It made the air fizz and sent an electric agony shooting up his arm, so that he staggered. "Watch it!" cried Melinda, running to him. "We don't know what kind of energy that is or what it can do."

Josh nodded, still rubbing his arm but pale with determination. "I know. I just thought… Maybe if we could understand the frequency—"

"We will," Melinda promised, her voice steely even though her eyes were clouded with doubt. "Just… Let's not get too close. We can't afford any accidents."

Throughout the night they made small but important discoveries: The portal seemed to be held open by certain geomagnetic anomalies native to the site which their tech had only compounded on; Professor Eldridge proposed a daring plan based on a little-known theoretical model that suggested they might be able to reverse the geomagnetic impact by creating a controlled electromagnetic pulse — a counter-surge that could potentially seal the portal.

The risks were enormous: The pulse could destabilize this area's natural magnetic field and screw with everything from wildlife navigation to local weather patterns. But then again — leaving a door open into a world we barely knew existed? That was not an option.

"Let's prepare very carefully," warned Eldridge, his voice heavy with how much was at stake in their decision. "This is not just about us or even this portal anymore; we are talking about affecting our environment at its most basic level."

As they began building said device capable of generating said pulse needed for said control over electromagnetism. They worked through shadows cast by falling dawn light looming out from behind them as if in reminder of what would follow failure toward completion under nervous tension born of proximity to unknown success within reach— or else.

Chapter 17:
Final Defense

The first light of morning made its way through the small windows at the top of the storage facility, weakly illuminating a crowded mess of scientific equipment and hastily drawn schematics. Josh, Melinda, and Professor Eldridge had gotten some sleep, but not much; they were too busy preparing for what they hoped would be their final confrontation with the portal. Anticipation hung thick in the air, mingling with the faint hum of electricity still coursing through the device they'd built — an intricate system of coils and wires and generators surrounding the modified core of the Phantom Cage, which was now designed to deliver a massive electromagnetic pulse.

Each member of the trio checked connections and rechecked them; moved with precision and methodical purpose. Melinda programmed a sequence into her laptop, typing it out with anxious speed. Professor Eldridge supervised — his eyes picking up calibration errors too small for anyone else to notice; his voice even but carrying an undercurrent of urgency.

"We have to make sure that this pulse is synchronized exactly with the portal's own frequency," he reminded them. "Any kind of mismatch could just make it worse."

Josh nodded, adjusted a dial on one of the generators. "How will we know if it's working?" he asked, wiping sweat from his brow with a shaky hand.

"We should see the portal start to contract — maybe even stop growing altogether," said Melinda without looking up from her screen. "The light inside should get dimmer too — or go out completely."

It was ready. They took cover behind heavy tables and metal cabinets; pulled goggles down over their eyes; felt their hearts pound against their chests like panicked fists. Melinda initiated a countdown on her laptop; began speaking seconds aloud in steady intervals.

"Three… two… one… activating now!"

She hit 'Enter' — and there was a deep thrumming power to everything suddenly; the floor beneath them shook. The air around the portal started to crackle with energy, and the light within it began to spin faster — not slower.

"It's resisting!" Professor Eldridge shouted over the noise; his words were nearly inaudible. "Increase the output!"

Josh adjusted a dial on one of the generators; pushed more power into the electromagnetic pulse. The light from the portal grew brighter — white and blinding, even behind their safety goggles.

Then — without warning — there was a shockwave. It hit them like a bus, knocked them off their feet: sent equipment flying through the air like missiles; shattered glass; twisted metal. They landed hard on their backsides, hearing ringing in their ears, seeing stars.

When they began to pick themselves up again — slowly, shakily; hearts still pounding — they saw that instead of closing up or going out as they'd hoped it would… The portal had just gotten larger. Its edges shimmered with violent agitation.

"They're not going back," Melinda gasped, staring at it in horror. "They're angry."

Shapes began to emerge from deep within its throbbing core then: coalescing out of light into forms that were simultaneously terrible and pitiful — figures twisted by pain and rage; faces contorted with terror or despair. A chorus of wails went up from all around them; filled the air until it felt solid enough to touch.

"We have to go," said Professor Eldridge firmly amid cacophony. "Now."

They stumbled back, tripping over the debris while spirits wailed around them. Leaving the storage facility, they saw the ground shaking beneath their feet and heard the building groaning like it was in pain.

Outside, they assembled themselves with heavy breaths and ruffled clothes against a backdrop of harsh morning light and failure. Behind them, the facility hummed with uncontrolled spectral energy as the dead screamed into the dawn.

While realizing that the portal is now more active than before and also more dangerous, they have to contain or find a way of escaping from what they had set free. As they collect themselves together again and strategize their next move under each one's weighty guilt in widening a rift between realms, can it ever be fixed?

With morning casting a weak light over everything in general but chaos specifically, Josh, Melinda, and Professor Eldridge stood far enough away from the storage facility for safety reasons; behind them jutted silhouetted figures against pale skies. The very structure seemed alive–unnaturally so–and pulsed with energy that made it groan under pressure from within. And out came sounds of tormented souls into empty space where no soul cared to listen.

The three were exhausted beyond description by this point; yet still not shaken enough considering all that's been done wrong here today alone. What used to seem like just another old cluster of buildings now appeared almost organic: alive but sickened with grief and rage which consumed its very being. Heat waves shimmered off walls thanks mostly due to visible air distortion caused by vibrating portal energy surrounding everything nearby; there also may have been some sunlight involved too probably though hard tell exactly how much since most would've been blocked out anyway given current circumstances etcetera blah blah blah.

"We can't leave it like this," Josh growled through clenched teeth as he stared at what should've been his own personal Chernobyl-verse glowing epicenter. "We've made everything worse. It's worse now because of us."

Leaning on a piece of debris while wiping his brow with a hand that shook despite its owner's best efforts, Professor Eldridge muttered, "I underestimated the strength of their connection… Those spirits trapped there; they're stronger than any I've ever encountered before – and more tortured too… This isn't just some breach between worlds; this is a wound. A deep festering wound."

Trying desperately to think through her fear, Melinda offered up another suggestion: "What about containment fields? If we can't close it then maybe we could keep it from spreading further?"

Taking time to consider all possibilities before speaking again, Professor Eldridge responded thoughtfully, "Yes… A containment field might work but only if powered by something far greater than what we currently possess… Even then however such an endeavor would be nothing more than temporary at best…"

As Josh and Melinda talked over their few remaining stratagems for saving world number one million three hundred fifty-seven thousand two hundred and eleven from certain doom according to theoretical calculations made last Tuesday afternoon around 3 PM give or take fifteen minutes due mainly in part thanks largely in whole entirely or partially solely etcetera blah blah blah yadda yadda yadda ad infinitum ad nauseam asinine adverbs inter alia ugh oh wait sorry wrong meeting anyway you get idea right well here she comes now folks brace yourselves boys girls ladies gentlemen children animals plants microbes viruses fungi slime molds etcetera please welcome our very own Dr Hailey Henley — physics department colleague specializing primarily (but not exclusively) within fields electromagnetic theory quantum mechanics relativity cosmology astronomy astrophysics exobiology extraterrestrial life forms astrobiology climatology meteorology geophysics environmental science ecology evolutionary biology paleontology archaeology history psychology sociology language literature mathematics computer programming engineering design optimization automation robotics artificial intelligence machine learning deep neural networks natural language processing data mining etcetera oh and she's also wicked good at making lasagna so there's that too I guess.

Josh stared at the figure standing on the edge of the facility, small and hunched. "What are you doing here?" he asked warily.

Dr. Henley came over, her eyes big with a mix of fear and scientific curiosity. "I heard the noise from my lab," she said nervously. "The energy readings I got were like nothing I've ever seen before. I had to see for myself."

She winced as she took in the scene before her. "This is bad, isn't it?" she asked, more a statement than a question.

"Very bad," Professor Eldridge said grimly. "We tried to close what we thought was a portal we'd opened, but instead…we seem to have made it stronger. More volatile."

Dr. Henley nodded, understanding the gravity of the situation. "I might be able to help," she offered after a thoughtful pause. "My research into electromagnetic stabilization could be adapted to create a containment field — at least strong enough to buy us time until we find something more permanent."

For just an instant Melinda's eyes flickered with hope. "Let's talk about this," she said, gesturing toward someplace safer than right next to an unstable building where reality was visibly unraveling around them. They convened in an outdated conference room on another part of campus; Dr. Henley spread out her notes and diagrams and explained her thoughts on creating a robust containment field.

As they begin hashing out specifics they are suddenly thrust into a new plan that might hold the spirits at bay; each person in the group has their own skill set or technical knowledge they bring forward as they work through the day on one thing: containing their mistake before something worse happens but it still feels like there's something else coming–a sense of dread hanging over every moment the portal remains active not just for them but for miles beyond these quiet university grounds.

The old conference room — rarely used for anything other than routine administrative meetings — became an essential war room; equations and diagrams hastily drawn up on the whiteboard, complex simulations humming through laptops. There was an urgency to the problem-solving now that Dr. Henley's specialized knowledge of electromagnetic fields was added to the mix.

With a calm precision that seemed impossible after everything we'd seen already today, Dr. Henley laid out her proposal for a containment field. "We can create a magnetic field strong enough to contain the portal within its current influence radius by using multiple high-output generators," she explained, indicating some calculations with her finger.

Professor Eldridge nodded slowly, his face lined with fatigue but his eyes bright with awakened curiosity — or maybe it was just hope; it had become hard to tell the difference anymore. "I had a similar theory years ago — but I didn't have anywhere near the level of technology required to test it. With your expertise and our firsthand knowledge of this portal…I think this might actually work."

Melinda, visibly exhausted but still sharp as ever, took in what he'd said and immediately began incorporating it into their plan. "We'll need to place the generators in very specific locations around the facility," she said, sketching a rough diagram of where things should go on one of the whiteboards lining the walls. "Each point needs to be calibrated so that its magnetic field overlaps with those from other generators at just the right strength to contain rather than exacerbate any energy coming out of or going into —" She stopped herself from getting too technical; Josh would understand what she meant.

Josh glanced up from his own list-making long enough to nod in agreement; he'd been busy reaching out across campus for help ever since we realized how far over our heads we were here. The good news was that everyone else could see exactly how dire things had gotten, too — red tape had been cut so many times today it felt like there must be miles of it strewn across these hallways right now; we'd secured commitments for everything from high-capacity power generators to advanced computing units necessary for monitoring the system — all we had to do now was make sure it worked.

The sun kept on rising, putting its blade-shadows in the empty rooms of the conference hall. The plan formed. Dr. Henley would deal with generator operations and Professor Eldridge with the magnetic field's theory and precision tuning. Melinda was going to figure out how to make that old portal data match up with this new containment strategy they'd come up with; she'd work on integrating them together somehow or another, but Josh? Josh had to keep everything moving at once – nobody else's job could be done if theirs wasn't first.

They knew just as well as anyone else did what was happening here today but still there seemed something almost cheerful about it all; maybe 'hopeful' is a better word though because hope implies action while cheerfulness suggests passivity so never mind then let's go back again: The mood inside those walls could have been called cautiously optimistic were it not for what hung over their heads – no, it wasn't just above us now either, it had fallen right down into our own laps too didn't it? We're not only fighting for our lives anymore are we? This thing has sucked us dry already and now we've got no choice left except try and stuff all its energy back in before it gets loose again – which means stuffing that whole damn world right along with us if necessary!

Everything became urgent after a while: nobody slept anymore; night fell hard around them like bricks stacked high against an open doorframe waiting for someone strong enough (or desperate enough) to shove 'em through. The equipment started showing up late afternoon-ish but by then people were running off adrenaline alone so who knows how long these things actually took or where they went after being dropped off at some makeshift storage facility marked "hazardous" in black spray paint letters half an inch tall?

As soon as they started testing those generators though… wow! You probably wouldn't believe this unless you saw it yourself – but there wasn't any sound except for those machines humming deep beneath our feet. It was like being inside an empty mountain range just before sunrise when all the streetlights turn on at once because some unlucky pedestrian happened to trip over a wire somewhere down the line; everything looked weirdly bright but not really natural light; more like if you took normal daylight and wrapped it up tight with barbed wire so it couldn't breathe anymore.

Right before they could start running that first test on containment though… right then, I swear on my mother's grave – this is what happened: The ground shook! Yes sir/madam/anyone else reading this now might want to sit down first, because yes indeed ma'am/buddy 'o mine: we had ourselves another earthquake! Only… it didn't feel quite as strong or long-lasting as ones usually do around here – thank god too because if anything had fallen off shelves during whatever kind of aftershocks might've come next? Well let me tell ya friend: ain't nobody got time for cleanin' up broken glass between two attempts at sealing up inter-dimensional rifts!

Anyway I'm getting off track again (story of my life huh?) so back to business: That portal thing lit up like July 4th fireworks on steroids! We were standing out in front of our command center when all this went down – you shoulda seen everyone's faces light right up along with those damn trees forty miles away from where we stood. The only thing brighter than either one? Both together!!

So now what?

Well now here's where things get real interesting don't, they though? Because from what I can figure out at least…the team just keeps pressing forward. Their eyes are set hard against something far beyond mere determination now -there isn't room left in there for anything less than full-on resolve while their hands steady themselves upon various switches and dials scattered across tables that have been pushed together haphazardly until they form an almost unbroken line leading straight back towards where we hope will be our final battleground against everything which should never have come through here in first place!!!!!!!!!!!!!

Chapter 18 :
The Fall of Melinda

On a gloomy day with continuous heavy rain, Melinda went to the edge of the cliff overlooking the stormy sea as she had been consumed by her thoughts due to immense grief and fear. Her whole personality which used to be methodical and composed was destroyed by their own self-inflicted supernatural powers plus guilt that hung over her.

Melinda wrapped herself in a thick jacket against the biting wind which kept blowing her hair into her face and took faltering steps down a rocky path towards the beach below. Overhead, the sky was filled with tumbling dark clouds that matched what was happening inside her mind. Step after step seemed only to steel her resolve — a tragic determination etched onto lips tightened and eyes gone far away.

Josh and Professor Eldridge felt an ache in their chests when they realized she wasn't at the makeshift command center. They remembered how distant she had been acting lately, those moments where they caught her staring into nothingness — when talk turned from scientific curiosity to existential dread. They called for her name while following behind them through opened spaces but could barely hear themselves think above all this howling wind mixed up with these crashing waves.

They found Melinda standing on the edge of a cliff overlooking a raging sea. She was dangerously close to falling off it, staring out into water with eerie calmness given context around her.

"Melinda!" Josh shouted in panic as he ran towards her along with Eldridge who was close behind him; however their words got swallowed by strong gusts blowing against them so that only sound reaching any ears there would have been louder than crashing waves beneath them.

She looked entranced, fixated upon some point far away beyond where dark ocean met stormy sky while every element nearby echoed inner turmoil which brought forth such madness – land versus sea, reality or oblivion?

A sudden gust whipped past Josh causing his heart to freeze; Melinda matched silhouette against boiling ocean waves behind her then stepped off into nothingness disappearing completely within blackness as she descended towards churning waters below.

This stopped both Josh and Eldridge dead in their tracks, hearts racing with equal parts disbelief and hopelessness as they reached edge. Peering down all that could be seen were shadows cast by moonlight mingling together with spray from furious sea crashing against jagged rocks.

Despite limited visibility coupled with dangerous conditions search started immediately; Coast Guard teams were called upon who risked lives navigating treacherous waters aboard boats or helicopters. They would not find her until first light of dawn painted pale somber hues over everything surrounding them.

Melinda's body had been discovered near base of cliff where it met water, battered beyond recognition throughout course its journey through unforgiving waves that were testament enough themselves to turbulent power possessed by such vast expanses. The tragic end for one so bright yet tortured seemed like blow felt hardest by everyone else involved and served only serve as reminder how much people paid when playing god.

Josh and Professor Eldridge, with the burden of taking Melinda back to the university upon them, know that they are facing reality. They must deal with their guilt and the insatiable need for answers about what happened to the rest of their colleagues who were haunted. Every decision they make as they prepare themselves for what should follow is informed by how much Melinda's death means to them—her passing away a ghost among them all, urging them on until they find closure in shutting down this gateway which takes innocent lives.

The morning sun rose above the horizon and cast a cold light on the tragic scene. The reality of Melinda's death settled over Josh and Professor Eldridge like a shroud. The Coast Guard recovery team worked efficiently and solemnly so that her body was not left behind in those turbulent waters where it had borne too violently testimony of sea's mercilessness.

The cliffs used to be an attractive site for many academics at the university but now bore signs of darkness; waves below constantly reminded everyone about what had happened during that dreadful night. Wrapped in official-looking plastic packaging, carried away from where she died by people who did not care much about who she was or what might have been going through her mind when such things occurred around him – even if anything did at all -, Josh could only stand still while looking at those fluctuating tides without saying a word because no words could explain how much they had lost.

When news got out about Melinda's demise within campus premises itself before spreading across other parts outside its borders where everyone knew each other either personally or professionally due to close interaction between lecturers/researchers/students etc., there arose clouds filled with sadness above heads hung low by sorrowful minds gathered together under one roof called love which was supposed bring people closer rather than pushing them apart especially when somebody dies unexpectedly leaving behind friends whom he/she has known since childhood days like brothers/sisters forevermore without saying goodbye forevermore until they meet again someday somehow somewhere sometime later in life.

In his office, Professor Eldridge sat with his head in hands. The weight of responsibility bore down on him. What were they going to do next? The portal was unstable still — it might even be more so now without Melinda's knowledge. He thought about their options; all fraught with danger and unknowns. They had to close that thing up soon or else there would only be more death but also everything would remain chaotic forever as an act of remembering her.

Josh returned back to the lab after spending hours by himself near where she drowned out at sea thinking deeply about what had occurred last night which haunted him deeply each time he tried putting thoughts into words while standing alone beside those turbulent waves crashing against jagged rocks below them; when he walked into the room – empty except for clutter left behind from when she hurriedly grabbed things off tables before running out -, it hurt too much seeing everything just how she'd left them knowing full well that never again will they work together towards solving puzzles which fascinated both equally much because such was this case now where every item reminds us not only our shared past but also present realities too.

Josh packed up her belongings: notebooks, laptop (still open) etc., each one another part of a day spent sharing ideas and experiments, trying desperately to figure out anything about what's happening around them – now all silent witnesses pointing back at himself as if saying "you should have done more." Determined not letting go but instead pushing forward through other members within department who can offer help when needed most especially since time seems like running out fast, determined not letting go but instead pushing forward through other members within department who can offer help when needed most especially since time seems like running out fast~

In the next days, there were some things that were done to put Professor Eldridge's containment plan in place. The lab was alive with activity, a sharp contrast to the recent solemn silence. Engineers and physicists worked side by side with ghost hunters, each bringing their expertise to bear on the new device — an updated Phantom Cage designed to trap and nullify the energy of the portal.

As they finished building it, Josh found himself standing before his assembled team. He looked out into their faces, etched in determination with just a touch of fear. Then he began to speak.

"We've lost someone incredible," he said, his voice thick with emotion. "Someone who lit up this lab every day with her brilliance. Melinda believed in what we do here; she believed we could make a difference. We owe it to her — and ourselves — not to let that end. Let's close this thing down and see that it never opens again."

Driven now by fresh inspiration and collective duty, the team readies itself for action. There is much at stake; they know this well enough. The burden upon them is heavy; danger lurks around every corner. But these are minor concerns at present. For now their hearts are filled only with memories of Melinda and thoughts of how she would have wanted things done. And so they work: long into nights made ever shorter by adrenaline rushes; fueled less by caffeine jitters than sheer force of willpower.

It's closing time. The portal must be sealed off forever. It's closing time.

The afternoon sun hung low over campus as the last words of Josh's speech echoed through otherwise silent halls. The whole world seemed frozen save for those within those walls. Too many had disappeared already. Melinda was just one more name on a list growing too long even for memory. She had died dreaming of alternate realities while living through ours. That couldn't be for nothing. Could it?

Thus newly inspired each member of the team busies themselves with preparations for leaving. The responsibility they bear now is great and so too are the risks. But Melinda's memory lives on in each one of them. They will do whatever it takes to ensure that every portal ever opened by man gets closed again.

The late afternoon sun cast long shadows across the lab. Each member of the team — now bolstered by Josh's speech — worked with a quiet intensity that filled the space. The stakes were clear, and though unspoken, anxiety hung heavy in the air; but so too did determination.

Their containment device, which they had begun calling “The Lock,” was a marvel of engineering and paranormal research. At its core, an intricate arrangement of electromagnetic coils and quantum stabilizers would create a field strong enough to trap and nullify the volatile energies associated with the phenomenon known as “the portal.” Around this core were protective barriers and fail-safes, layer after layer; each added complexity also added strength.

Professor Eldridge oversaw final assembly. Adjusting his glasses as he examined each connection and component, he reminded his team: “Precision is key here; any deviation could worsen instability.”

Melinda’s workspace — now occupied by her closest colleagues — became ground zero for all computational work needed to control The Lock. Her notes were kept; her algorithms formed foundational basis for software designed to run device operations. And thus she continued.

As night fell over campus, casting twilight into lab rooms already dim from overhead fluorescents flickering against dying daylight hours, there was a pause. A momentary break in routine. Not one meant for rest or respite no. This brief hiatus came about solely because certain initial power-up sequence tests required it. There would be time enough later for sighs and further hesitations. Now only action mattered. In that moment what everyone heard most clearly was not some imagined click or beep signaling success but rather — almost imperceptibly at first — faint hum of The Lock coming to life.

However, during the last adjustments before they can be deployed something unusual happened. A sudden change in energy readings almost stopped the work on the spot. Dr Henley frowned at the screen showing data that was supervised by Josh, “We’re observing a raise in quantum flux measurements. It’s small but it might indicate an instability within the field matrix”. The voice of him was rather nervous.

Dr Henley narrowed her eyes and said: “Let’s recalibrate flux capacitors and run sequence again. No uncertainty is allowed”.

The process of recalibration had to be done carefully because there were many tiny components as well as big ones which should be taken into account simultaneously while making any changes since otherwise system could collapse very easily. Up until dawn they worked with computer screens shining on their faces and sparks from The Lock flying off every now and then when somebody adjusted something in it.

There was silence outside where normally night-time hustle and bustle reigned supreme – everybody knew how serious things were going inside that remote laboratory. The team moved around like ghosts haunted not only by their professional reasons but also driven personally to make good whatever had gone wrong with reality to shreds it had been torn apart at.

In those early hours of morning fatigue mingled with determination – all preparations for deployment were being finalized now; soon enough The Lock would be ready for its installation at portal site; optimism prevailed among these people who knew better than anyone else what still lay ahead during next few hours; however everyone felt uneasy about what these final steps might unleash upon world again

Epilogue:
The Aftermath

Several months had passed since the team's last-ditch effort to close the portal at Whitmore Asylum. Winter had come and gone, leaving behind only a few dirty piles of snow that lined the streets of spring. But for now, a cold quiet lay over everything — a stillness befitting the ruins of an old asylum.

Buried deep in the rubble of what was once ground zero for all things haunted and horrifying, The Lock and other experimental technologies sat hidden, forgotten. They rested beneath fallen beams and shattered concrete — human ambition turned to dust and twisted metal. But not all forces slept — while contained for now by The Lock, the portal simmered with power restrained; its presence stained the world darkly.

In a nondescript suburban house miles away from this desolation, a teenager's smartphone buzzed with a notification. He picked it up curiously; his eyes went wide as he saw what it was. An app — one he didn't remember downloading — displayed a cryptic message on its splash screen: "See Beyond the Veil." This was it: overnight reinstalled mysteriously icon'd eye within pentagram'd app.

And then across town this started happening everywhere else too: phones buzzing in busy office buildings next to laptops where they sat open on important documents; phones buzzing in silent libraries next to stacks of books about ghosts no one else believed in but that still made them shiver when they were alone at night; phones buzzing in bustling marketplaces next to tables piled high with fruits and vegetables grown from soil that had seen more death than life; phones buzzing in serene homes where people thought themselves safe because they'd never been touched by death.

Around the globe, these notifications began occurring simultaneously on devices new and old. It spread silently but swiftly like a virus leaping from host to host without leaving any trace of where it came from or how it got there.

At the university, Josh sat in his office lined with books on paranormal phenomena and quantum physics. His phone buzzed on the desk. He picked it up, saw the screen and felt his gut sink. The app was there. It beckoned. Letting the phone drop like it burned him, he leaned back in his chair, mind racing. "It's starting again," he whispered to himself as a cold dread settled deep in his chest.

In another part of the world, Professor Eldridge received a similar notification on his tablet. Now retired, now far away from that terrifying portal — but still this message: so clear; so terrifying; about what they thought they'd buried; about what they thought they could forget; about what refused to be silenced; about how something found another way out; about how something had adapted and evolved beyond their control.

Melinda's old colleagues — those who had taken up her mantle and continued researching spectral phenomena — convened an emergency meeting. A live data feed from around the world showed on the screen at one end of the room: reports of the app appearing en masse along with unexplained events and an uptick in spectral sightings.

"The cycle hasn't ended," said one researcher grimly. "It's moved … past any one place now."

The team looked at each other across a heavy silence, realizing all too well what this meant for them — for their responsibility to find some kind of answer. Ideas were tossed around with increasing desperation — global digital strikes, mass public awareness campaigns, partnering with tech giants to somehow purge this thing from existence once and for all …

Having said their goodbyes, the research team left the meeting room with even more questions than answers. They were given an impossible task. The world had changed, a shift so subtle it was hardly noticeable, but one that drew a line across everything we knew and dropped us right into the deep end of what we didn't.

Night fell outside. The sky was clear—the stars bright, inescapable—and people everywhere looked at their phones.

They glanced at them in city streets and suburban neighborhoods, in overcrowded apartments and houses perched on empty cul-de-sacs; they glanced at them in neon-lit bars and flickering subway cars; they glanced at them on park benches as dogs strained against leashes to sniff around dirty sidewalks; they glanced at them walking down corridors lined with closed bedroom doors where teenagers sat hunched beneath comforters watching YouTube videos about conspiracy theories; they glanced at them while lying alone in bed as white ovals floated behind their eyelids.

The app blinked up from dark screens, its symbol simple yet enigmatic: a spiral within a circle within a square. It appeared without fanfare or notification—simply there one second when it wasn't before—and it launched itself when no fingers touched its icon.

Unseen and unheard, something beyond crossed its legs and smiled.

This is not how stories end.

The battle may have been lost for now, but the war wages on. We contained the portal this time, but who knows where it will open next? The next chapter is yet unwritten but inevitable. The world changed tonight—that much is certain—but whether it ends in apocalypse or revelation remains to be seen.

Around three o'clock in the morning Berlin time—a sleepless night for many—a university student named Leyla noticed her phone lighting up across the room. She watched as the app opened itself on her screen: a digital eye that pulsed hypnotically. Her own eyes widened. The clock on her bedside table began to flicker, its numbers distorting as if they were being reflected in water. Leyla felt something cool and light pass by her—an exhale of air too quick for breath.

In a crowded café in Tokyo, a businessman's phone did the same thing. He picked it up just as his coffee cup rattled against its saucer—just once, but enough for him to notice. A low and distant vibration hummed through the device and into his hand. People around him looked away from each other and down at their phones, swiping and tapping with sudden unease.

At the university, Josh had called an emergency meeting with what was left of the original research team plus some new recruits from digital forensics and cybersecurity. They gathered around a large monitor that displayed a world map covered in red dots: app appearance; associated paranormal activity.

"It's not an app," one of the cybersecurity guys said, a little too loudly over his coffee-stained mask. "It's a trigger." He tapped at clusters—ley lines or fault lines or whatever started to form patterns when you squinted right—that pulsed across the screen like nerve endings snapping shut.

Professor Eldridge appeared via video call from quarantine in Ohio.

"We thought we closed a door," he said quietly from inside his square on the monitor, "but maybe all we did was open a window."

His voice was flat—a graveyard man stacking regrets—but there was no need to lean on inflection here; every syllable rung with failure.

"A window that can't be shut by conventional means."

While discussing possible answers – from trying to hack the app in large numbers to launching an educational campaign about it – the room's lights flickered, a physical reminder that what they were up against was not just digital. The digital forensics expert quickly isolated the code on her laptop, her fingers dancing across the keyboard. "There's something here — codes within codes; like it's evolving or…" Read more: https://www.dailycal.org/2022/04/27/transcendence/#more-516331

Josh stood behind her as lines of code scrolled past. "Can you trace where it came from?" he asked, a sense of urgency in his voice.

"It's like chasing smoke," she said without taking her eyes off the screen. "But there's a pattern; a signature that keeps repeating. It almost feels like… a call."

The implications were chilling. The app wasn't merely their unsuccessful containment — it was alive and growing, reaching out across the digital ether, calling into whatever lay beyond the portal.

At first light, with dawn creeping through the windows of the lab, nobody spoke for some time as each member of the team considered what they had learned. Outside, people went about their morning routines unaware that there was a ghost in every machine around them; an entity that had grown beyond its beginnings.

About the Author

Bennard Terrell is a writer who loves to travel and loves writing equally. He takes his readers on trips that defy imagination. He has always managed to keep his audience spellbound through skillfully telling stories with interesting structures.

His writings are an expression of a life fully lived and closely observed; thus, they form a rich tapestry of experiences reflected by different characters and places. Realistic cultural representations as well as profound human realities have been included in his novels due to the fact that Bennard studied anthropology and traveled worldwide.

Every new publication should not just narrate but also kindle people's own curiosity according to Bennard Terrel while drawing him closer towards achieving self-discovery through literature. Love for enigmas surrounding our existence permeates through all his narratives which are delivered in an eloquent prose understandable by everyone without exception; hence, it can be said that individuals do not only read them but also live them.

As one goes from page after another on this book recently offered for sale, there must be preparedness for shifting into totally strange or wholly recognizable environments alike—because he thinks every single published work represents nothing less than communication between writers themselves as well readers like us; even more so when such authors write sincerely hoping their words touch us deeply somewhere inside our hearts where feelings reside forevermore until death shall separate these two souls bound together forevermore during eternity itself too if need be…

The End

www.ingramcontent.com/pod-product-compliance
Lightning Source LLC
LaVergne TN
LVHW010103170826
845678LV00012B/2224

* 9 7 8 2 9 9 8 3 1 2 0 2 0 *